CITY SHIF

BOOK 2

Chasing Trouble

LAYLA NASH

Cover design by
Resplendent Media

Interior book design by
Write Dream Repeat Book Design LLC

chapter I

Benedict hated getting up early on his day off. He'd been looking forward to a lazy Friday of sweatpants, grilled cheese sandwiches, and beer. Until Atticus called. From jail.

He gritted his teeth as he strode into the reception area. It would take a couple of hours to sort this all out, though Benedict didn't have his hopes up. Atticus hadn't been particularly forthcoming about what led to his arrest, and the sullen "I don't knows" felt more like teenage angst than what a goddamn man would own up to.

Benedict knew the clerks and bailiffs at the jail and the courthouse, and smiled and joked about being there on unofficial official business as the morning ticked away. All while wanting to punch Atticus in the face the moment he saw him. The feeling intensified when he paid out the ten thousand dollar bond to the clerk, gritting his teeth as he imagined all the ways to make Atticus pay it back. Son of a bitch.

The deputies brought Atticus out and for a moment Benedict couldn't speak — his little brother looked like hell warmed over, even with their supernatural healing ability. Bruises and lumps covered his face and at least two massive cuts had butterfly bandages holding them together. Benedict raised his eyebrows as he pointed Atticus into the corner. "Over there. Sit."

Atticus scrubbed a hand over his short hair, holding his bag of belongings from the property locker. "Can't we do this at home? I feel like shit."

"You look worse, and we're doing this here so I can decide what to tell Logan." Benedict scanned the handful of other people waiting in the reception area; all human, nothing to worry about. He loomed over Atticus as the younger man flopped into a flimsy plastic chair that creaked dangerously under his weight. "What the fuck is wrong with you?"

"There was a fight, the cops showed up, I tried to shift and get away but ended up naked in an alley. They used their imaginations. Nothing I could do about it."

"Why the fuck were you naked in an alley?" Benedict heard a snort behind him and lowered his voice, fury swelling his shoulders as the lion wanted to burst forth and teach his brother a lesson.

Atticus shrugged, not meeting his gaze but staring past Benedict at the door. A muscle jumped in his jaw, just under a thick white scar from his ear to his throat. "It just happened."

Benedict massaged his temples and turned away for a moment so he wouldn't grab the kid by the throat and throw him across the room. *It just happened.* It always just happened around Atticus. It was the fourth time in as many months that he'd been arrested for fighting, or public nudity, or any number of minor crimes. Enough that Logan was starting to get pissed.

Benedict took a deep breath and faced his brother. "You have got to get this under control. I don't know what the fuck you're doing, Atticus, but clean it up. Got me?"

"I get it." The sullenness faded to fatigue, and for a moment Benedict saw his brother exhausted, beaten. Broken. Atticus gingerly put his head in his hands. "I don't know if I can stop."

"We'll figure it out." Benedict didn't fully understand what the problem was, just that his brother needed help. Something was seriously wrong, and if —

He turned as slow-moving chaos burst into the reception area, two patrol cops wrestling with a kid and getting a little too rough. Benedict frowned, gesturing at his brother to get up and handing him the keys. "Let's get you some food and —"

"I'm innocent," the kid yowled, and the hair stood up on Benedict's arms. His vision narrowed, focused on the kid, and he saw her face. Not a kid, a young woman. Being manhandled far too roughly, unprofessionally, by two cops who enjoyed it a bit too much. She looked ill, weak, and kept her eyes screwed shut as she struggled. "Let me go, you're not supposed to —"

"Shut the fuck up," one of the cops said, grabbing a fistful of her hair and knocking the girl over one of those damn plastic chairs.

Atticus bristled, growled a little, and Benedict shoved him at the door. "I'll handle it, you don't need to get arrested again. *Go.*"

And Benedict strode forward. "Hey! Get your hands off my client before I file excessive force and brutality complaints."

The cops scowled but eased up; one held the girl's upper arm as the other handed the arrest paperwork to booking. One muttered, "Your client? She must account for half your salary."

"Unhand my client." Fear rolled off the girl in waves and riled up his lion, along with the cruelty emanating from the cops. Benedict had a healthy respect for the police but wouldn't tolerate the occasional bad seeds that turned up in their line of work. He looked past the cops at the booking agent and tilted his head at a few chairs in a more private corner. "Do you mind if I speak with my client briefly? We'll be filing the bail agreement shortly."

The clerk smiled, clicking away at the computer. "Of course, Benedict. We'll have her processed lickety-split."

"Good." He caught the girl's elbow and pulled her away from the handsy cop, scowling at the dick as they moved away. In the corner, Benedict put the girl in one of the chairs and placed himself between her and the cops, so they couldn't see her and she couldn't see them. He kept his voice low enough they wouldn't overhear. "What's your name?"

"Eloise."

Her voice was low and throaty, and she kept her eyes on the floor. A frisson of interest, of curiosity, ran through him. The tone in her voice, the smell of her skin, and the crackle in the air around her meant non-human. Definitely something supernatural, but she didn't smell like a lion or a wolf or any shifter he knew. He took a deep breath near her and the girl went still, sliding a glance at him. Ice blue eyes, almost silver, slid across his face and then back to the floor. They hit him like a punch in the gut, and he forgot, for a moment, where he was.

He shook himself back to reality. Time was limited and he had to get her away from the jail before she ended up booked all weekend. "I'm Benedict. I'll be your lawyer for the time being, at least until we can get you out of here."

"Great." She picked at a loose thread on her jeans, hands nervous despite the handcuffs restraining her.

"What did they pick you up for?"

She made an odd noise in her throat, almost a laugh, but shrugged instead. "They didn't really say."

Irritated, Benedict spun on his heel and confronted the cops. "What are the charges against my client?"

The taller cop, unimpressed, raised his eyebrows and handed over a copy of the arrest sheet. "Oh, you know. Small potatoes. Illegal betting, book making, money laundering, fraudulent wire transfers, and some racketeering."

"Racketeering?" Benedict took the paper but didn't look away from the cop. "Are you fucking kidding me? Does she look capable of racketeering?" And he flung his arm back at the girl, who blinked and looked around as if confused why she was even at the jail.

The short cop snorted, an ugly sound. "Look, friend, you don't know your client very well. We've arrested her at least ten times this year alone. Theft, transporting stolen goods, forgery, obstructing an official investigation, breaking and entering... You're not getting out of this shit," and he pointed at Eloise behind Benedict. "These are federal charges, sweetheart, so you best pay your lawyer however you can."

And the sneer on his face left little doubt how he thought Eloise paid him. Benedict's blood ran cold with rage and his lion roared in the back of his head, ready to pounce. But he kept his face expressionless as he looked at the patrol cops. "If you have any issues, address them to me. My client will not be speaking with you further."

He looked at the girl and the curtain of dark hair hiding her expression. He dropped his voice again as the cops headed for the door. "Forgery? Really?"

A hint of a smile, quickly hidden. "No idea what they're talking about."

Benedict snorted, about to go back to the clerk to resolve the bail, then leaned down to try to see her face. "Who are your people?"

She went very still. Her gaze slowly lifted to his face and Benedict rocked back on his heels; definitely supernatural. Had to be. Her eyes were gray-silver with hints of blue, flecks of lightning through the irises. Enthralling. Devastating.

She cleared her throat. "I'm Eloise. That's it."

A mystery. His lion perked up. He grinned, patted her shoulder. "What are you doing for lunch?"

chapter 2

I made a lot of noise as the cops dragged me into booking, but in reality, I looked forward to a quiet weekend at the jail. No one would bother me, meals came on time and were generally edible, and I could finally get some sleep. Besides, one of my runners was in jail and I needed to get her a message.

And then some knight in shining armor showed up, claiming to be my lawyer, and yelled at the cops when they got a little handsy. I knew better than to argue, but I didn't dare look at him too directly. He was good-looking enough my mojo would decide for itself to ensnare him, and I didn't need that complication. Already I was late for my meeting with Val, and she didn't like being ignored. The matriarch of the hyena shifters didn't get to the head of the pack by being a nice or patient person.

I chewed the inside of my cheek and concentrated on the location of the knight's highly-polished, ridiculously expensive leather shoes. A man with money. So definitely not a public defender. His watch said the same thing as he paused in front of me, his voice deeper than I expected. "What are you doing for lunch?"

Startled, I looked at him. "What?"

His eyes, a swirl of brown and gold, caught me. Held me captive, and warmth surged through my chest. Holy shit. He was too handsome for his own good, clean shaven with striking cheekbones and a strong jaw that implied stubbornness. And trouble. Way too much trouble, by the way his light brown hair fell across his forehead. He was used to getting his way. But he held out a hand. "I can hear your stomach growling, Ms. Eloise. Let's get a sandwich. I know a nice bistro, right around the corner."

Against my better judgment — but more because those damn cops still loitered nearby and would no doubt follow me down the street to pin some other bogus crimes on me — I got up and shoved my hands in my pockets. "Sure."

"Great." His hand slid around my elbow as he led the way out of booking, while he waved and called his thanks to the clerk behind the counter. But the look he gave the cop was straight out death. When we were outside and he started leisurely toward an unknown destination, he released my arm and took his own casual posture. "My name is Benedict, by the way."

"Great," I said, echoing him. Men liked that, usually. Pretend like their words were more powerful than my own. It became habit. I rubbed my nose and glanced over my shoulder, where that goddamn cop followed, half a block back. Looking suspicious as hell. I scanned the street for his partner, knowing those two in particular never worked alone. "Thanks for the bail and everything, it's totally a bum rap and —"

"Don't worry about it." This Benedict character had an easy smile, glancing at me as he paused next to a restaurant and opened the door. "I'm glad I could help. Please," he said, and gestured inside.

It was not, in any sense of the word, a bistro. Maybe if bistro really meant over-priced, hoity-toity, totally unafford-able and uncomfortable with cloth table cloths, waiters that put the napkin in your lap for you, and too many utensils to know when to use what. I balked in the doorway. "You can't be serious."

"You don't like this place?" His eyebrows arched, then he looked down the street. "There's a couple —"

"It's..." I took a deep breath then shrugged. Why the fuck not. "Sure. I normally try not to spend more than a hundred bucks on lunch, but what the hell."

His head tilted, a half-smile making him more handsome. "There's a taco truck across the street, but their wine selection is terrible."

I laughed as I looked at him. I didn't mean to do either, but he surprised me. Imagine, a lawyer with a sense of humor. His teeth flashed white and a little pointy as he ushered me into the restaurant, his hand low on my back. Shivers raced through me and I concentrated on the floor. Keep it together, Eloise. Keep it together.

Benedict greeted the suited waiter dude at the front like they were old friends, and instead of waiting like a couple of other schmucks in the lobby, he showed us to a small table near the window immediately. Benedict pulled out a chair for me, though I fidgeted and wanted to take the other chair — it had a good view of the door and the kitchen, and its back to a wall. But he obviously wanted the superior ground, so I caved and sat, feeling twitchy with my back to the door and any threat that might come sauntering in. Like those fucking cops. Maybe they worked for Val.

I chewed my lip as I checked my phone; no missed calls just yet, but that didn't mean anything. I wasn't late yet.

Benedict said something to a waiter who approached while I was busy looking over my shoulder, and before I could decipher what he ordered, the waiter disappeared. Benedict smiled, disarmingly boyish. "So, Eloise. What do you do for a living?"

And again he surprised me into laughing. I chewed my lip but refused to look at him, not wanting him to see my eyes. "What do you think?"

Long, thin fingers drummed on the pristine tablecloth. "Kindergarten teacher?"

I smiled, looked away. A joker. "Try again."

"Sunday school teacher?"

"Not even close."

He made a thoughtful noise, eyes sparkling when I dared glance at him. "A judge, then. Clearly."

I snorted, about to fire back about the legal profession when the waiter returned with a bottle of wine. Benedict studied the label, nodded, and went through a whole ritual with smelling the cork, swirling and tasting the wine, then finally giving permission to the waiter to pour for me. And he did it without a hint of pretension. Until he caught sight me of staring at him, and laughed. "What?"

"I've never seen anyone do that in real life," I said, shifting in the chair. The sooner this ended, the sooner I could get some place to wash the sludge from the cop car off me and get some rest before I faced Val and her minions. I'd already missed the meeting, and Val wouldn't be happy with my absence or the failed ransom drop.

"I'm glad you're impressed." He smiled, though a puzzled frown replaced it after a few moments. "So about those charges they threw at you. Any truth to them?"

"Who, me?" I affected a wide-eyed innocent look, gasping at the sheer audacity of him implying anyone like me could possibly be engaged in any such nefarious activities. "That's the most ludicrous —"

He laughed, holding up his hands to cut me off. "Okay, okay. Forgery, huh?" He made a thoughtful noise, then snorted. "I've never had a forger before. This should be interesting." He pulled a card from inside his suit coat and handed it to me. "I'm not a criminal attorney by day, but I'll offer pro bono defense services, if you need them."

"Thought all lawyers were criminals," I said under my breath, but put the card in my pocket for later. Just in case. "But thanks."

The waiter returned to list the specials, and when I looked at Benedict with a hint of panic, he winked and said, "Hope you don't mind if I order for both of us?" and then proceeded to do so. After the waiter departed, he picked up his glass of wine and leaned back. "Hope you like snails."

"Damn, I just had that yesterday."

I liked him. Medusa strike me down, I liked him. He was funny and charming and surprisingly unpretentious about himself and the restaurant and everything. And he made me laugh.

He carried the conversation as the waiter brought out round after round of food — soup and salad and bread and some weird appetizer and then an artsy construction of chicken and vegetables that tasted good even if I couldn't have named any of the ingredients other than chicken. And part of me mourned that this had to be a one-time thing, despite the business card burning a hole in my pocket. I wouldn't call him. He might have the paperwork from the jail, but the only truthful information on it was my first name. I could disappear and Val would take care of those particular charges. She'd better. She owed me.

Benedict's easy smile coaxed another laugh from me, and maybe even a blush. I passed a hand over my eyes, not daring look at him too closely. He spoke into his wine glass, though his blue eyes twinkled. "You should smile more, Eloise. You light up when you smile."

And that time I definitely blushed. Turned to smile out the window instead, and went still as I caught sight of one of Val's enforcers, prowling around. Maybe looking for me. I swallowed hard, turning back to ask him for a ride or a hand or a new life, maybe.

But he held up his ringing phone, "Excuse me for a moment, I need to take this," and headed toward the quieter entry area.

I leaned in my chair and lifted the wallet from his back pocket, pretending to search my bag for something when he glanced back. I almost felt bad. He strode off, talking and gesturing widely as whoever on the other side of that call pissed him off. That was my cue. The wallet was fine leather, maybe sharkskin or ostrich skin or something really creepy, and fat with cash and cards. I dropped it in my bag and patted my mouth with the napkin before easing up from my chair. When his back was turned, I headed for the ladies' room. Another turn by the kitchen and a back door via the employee break room opened up ahead of me, and I slid out into a back alley that stank of garbage. There was always a back alley.

I checked my watch as I jogged to the main street and tried to blend into the crowds going about their afternoon business. The money drop didn't go well and Val would be looking for a scapegoat. I called Lacey but she didn't pick up, and I frowned. We'd had a deal — Lacey and her boyfriend would pick up the money for a fresh start somewhere else, and then Lacey would call her mother before Val really flipped her shit. Twelve hours later, and nothing. No money, no call, no Lacey. My stomach twisted and I glanced over my shoulder.

I reeked of cop car and jail and that lawyer, and no way could I go home. I headed for one of the shadier parts of the city and silenced my phone. There were a few hiding places yet that Val didn't know about. Or so I hoped.

chapter 3

Edgar laughed from the moment he stepped into the restaurant to pay Benedict's bill, he laughed the entire ride to the Chase Company's main office building, and he laughed the long elevator ride up to the security office. Benedict fumed. Calling his brother for help since his wallet mysteriously disappeared was humiliating enough, but knowing a girl managed to pick his pocket without him knowing was what really burned his pride.

Edgar at least waited until the door to his office closed behind them and he occupied the chair behind his desk to start asking questions. "Who is she?"

"How do you know it's a she?"

His older brother cocked an eyebrow at him. Benedict made an aggravated noise and threw his hands in the air. "Fine. Her name is Eloise."

"Eloise." Edgar smiled a little as he checked his computer, attention only partly on his brother. "And how did you meet young Eloise?"

Benedict gritted his teeth. "At the jail, when I was bailing Atticus —"

Edgar's chair squeaked as he swiveled to face Benedict, and he folded his arms on the desk with a blank expression. "Bailing Atticus out? Little brother was in jail?"

"Yes." Benedict went to the window and stared out at the city. Somewhere down there, Eloise had his wallet and his credit cards, doing God only knew what with his money. He hoped she bought something nice with it, something she wanted. He shoved his hands in his pockets. "It's fine. I bailed him out, we pled down with the judge and he's on the hook for some community service."

"The charges?"

"Fighting and public nudity." Benedict snorted, turning to face his brother. "Sounds like a hell of a Thursday night, right?"

Edgar's expression didn't change. The silence stretched. After a long, uncomfortable staring contest, Edgar made a note on a pad of paper and gestured with his hand. "And what was your girl charged with?"

A sudden urge to protect her washed over Benedict and he dissembled, shrugging as he wandered around the pristine security office to consider the bay of monitors. "Illegal gambling, I think it said. She placed some bets and got caught. Nothing too serious."

"And your natural response was to take her to lunch? To Bistro Nord?"

He watched the small, smudged figures moves through the monitors, all of them going about their business with purpose and vigor. It was his day off, he should have gone home and taken a nap, watched some of his recorded shows. Instead he wanted to search the city for Eloise. "She was hungry. I fed her."

Edgar took a deep breath, exhaling in a gust. "Okay. Where would she go?"

"No idea." Benedict shook his head, arms folded across his chest. "It's fine, Ed. If it's meant to be, our paths will cross again."

His brother leveled a look at him that put Benedict back a step. Edgar picked up his phone and dialed, still watching Benedict as the phone rang. At length, the security chief said, "I need to track down a few things. Benedict's wallet, to start. Credit cards. Yes. Top priority."

Benedict frowned. "You don't have to —"

Edgar leaned back in his chair, tossing a stress ball from hand to hand. His dark eyebrows arched as he spun the chair back and forth. "Someday you'll thank me."

"See, every other time you've said that to me, I haven't."

"This time is different."

"Why do you think that?" Benedict looked back at the monitors.

"Because I know you." Edgar laughed. "And you haven't made a joke since I picked you up, despite this being the funniest thing that ever happened to you."

"I don't find anything at all funny about this," Benedict said, trying to preserve some of his dignity. He drew his shoulders back, prepared to face his judgmental older brother when something thumped into the back of his head. The stress ball dropped to the floor and rolled across the industrial carpet. He scowled as Edgar grinned and spun in his chair. "You're enjoying this too much."

"Are you kidding me?" The phone rang and Edgar picked it up, still smiling. "This is the most fun I've had since Logan got all respectable. But don't think we won't talk about Atticus." Then he was embroiled in an intense conversation, and Benedict retrieved the stress ball to chuck back at him.

They threw things at each other until Edgar ran out of loose items on his desk and Benedict retreated to a firing position behind the ratty couch, though Edgar continued his reasonable phone call and Benedict's aim suffered from thoughts of Eloise. At least she'd eaten a good meal before she ran.

As the sun set and the temperature dropped, he hoped she was some place warm and comfortable. His apartment — and his bed — would have been the best option, but she hadn't given him the chance to offer. He dodged a tape dispenser as it sailed over the couch and crashed against the coffee table, and popped his head up to frown at Edgar and shake his finger. "You're going to —" but he hit the deck as a keyboard followed.

"Don't make me tell Logan." Edgar hung up, then cursed and flopped under his desk as Benedict heaved an armful of crap back at him and shrapnel fell across the glass contraption. The security chief straightened, running a hand through his hair. "Do you want to know where she is, or not?"

"What the hell am I going to do, go pick her up? Demand my wallet back?"

Edgar glanced at his watch, arching his eyebrows. "Well, it's just about dinner time —" and laughed as Benedict heaved a chair at him.

But Benedict bit back a smile as Edgar handed over a piece of paper with an address, a hotel where she'd used his credit card. The chase. His heart sped up, the blood pumping in his veins as the lion awoke and sensed a new hunt. Delicious prey. The chance for a reward at the end of the run. He straightened his tie, checked his hair in the reflection of one of the security monitors, and turned toward the door. "Great. I'll call you tomorrow if —"

"Hold up."

Benedict turned, not about to put up with more teasing when Eloise waited for him in a shitty neighborhood. "Enough with the —" but he cut off when he saw Edgar holding up a black canvas wallet. Benedict swallowed his pride and strode to take the jump wallet, laden with cash and a company credit card.

Before he released it, though, Edgar said quietly, not a hint of jest in his eyes, "Be careful, Ben. The kind of girl you bail out on a first date might not be the kind of girl you want her to be. Stalk the gazelle before you commit and find a fucking rhinoceros, okay?"

Benedict met his gaze, unafraid. "She's different. Special. There's something about her eyes..." He shook his head, unable to explain the silver lightning that struck right in his heart.

"Okay." Edgar released the wallet and turned his full attention to the computer, shaking his head. "Just call the house and make sure Natalia doesn't make a plate for you."

Benedict waved over his shoulder as he headed for the elevators. Fair warning from his older brother, certainly, but the hunt was on.

chapter 4

The hotel did enough questionable business that the front desk clerk didn't blink when I handed her a man's card, with no man in tow. She just swiped it and handed it back, smacking her gum loudly before pointing at the hall behind her and handing over an actual key with a giant wooden keychain attached to it. "One night, honey. Be out by 11 tomorrow morning. Ice machines on each floor, near the stairs. You're on the second floor, back corner."

"Thanks." I took the key and ran, careful to keep my head tilted down so the security camera behind her wouldn't get my face. I needed a baseball hat or something, but going home to get a change of clothes meant picking up some of Val's watchdogs, no doubt. So I'd settled for helping myself to new clothes, although they were new from the thrift store. Another place that didn't care if I used my 'brother's' credit card.

The room wasn't particularly clean, but it would work for a night. I showered in the lukewarm water, though I kept my socks on to avoid a suspiciously fuzzy tile floor, and debated taking a nap before facing Val. The queen of the hyenas was not someone to face at less than your personal best, and I needed rest before I could un-fuck whatever went wrong with the ransom trade. I checked my phone again as I dried my hair with a white rag that might once have been a towel, but resembled something closer to sandpaper as it tangled around my head. No calls from Lacey, but no calls from Val, either.

As I paced and debated what to do, that damn lawyer's face kept distracting me. And his laugh, and the smile, and the twinkle in his eyes, and the way his hands flexed on the table like he wanted to hold my hand. My stomach tightened as I thought of him, and I readjusted the towel before digging through the bag of clothes. I didn't believe in buying thrift store underwear so my own would have to do; inside-out was better than someone else's drawers.

Benedict. What a ridiculous name.

I groaned and put my hands over my face. I couldn't afford the distraction. Val would find me, she would absolutely hunt me down, and then I would have to answer for what happened to her daughter. Even if it was totally, unequivocally not my fault.

It sure as shit was the last time I did Lacey a favor.

Chewing my lip, I dressed in jeans and t-shirt and hoodie. Everything dark and kind of bulky, so hopefully no one would recognize or remember me. My hair was still wet but it went up in a bun, out of the way. Everyone always remembered the hair. Thick ropes of dark, glossy glamour, as Mum used to say. Luring men to their doom, entangling them until their lives were forfeit. Every time I cut off the damn locks, they grew back overnight, just as long. All I'd ever wanted was a bob, or cute bangs, or — God forbid — a pixie cut.

God damn Gorgons. I gritted my teeth and shoved my own clothes into the shopping bag and shoved it behind a chair. But you couldn't run from blood. Gran said that, not Mum. Mum tried to run and it hadn't worked out for any of us. I had to reach Lacey, had to figure out what the fuck was going on before I faced her mother. And since Val could probably track my phone, I needed a pay phone. I slung my bag over my shoulder, threw open the door, and bit back a curse, rocking back on my heels.

Val, grizzled face more sour than usual, stood in the hall, flanked by two of her other daughters. "Eloise."

"Uh, Val." I stepped back so they could come in, though I glanced up and down the hall behind them to double check. Yep, two more daughters guarding the stairs, and another at the only viable window. Definitely not getting away unless Val said so. I cleared my throat and closed the door, though I didn't set the chain. Just in case I needed to get out in a hurry. I could deal with the ones in the hall, but my scary mojo generally didn't work on someone as tough as Val. "I was just going to look for you."

"Right." The queen of the hyenas looked like a tough version of every television grandma, her hair mostly white but cut short and spiked up in an aggressive style, and her cold brown eyes tracked me as I sauntered into the room and leaned against the wall. Even a foot shorter than me, she managed to loom menacingly from the door. "What happened?"

"I dropped the money exactly where you told me," I said. My phone charged on the table next to the bed, behind her.

I'd never reach it in time. The window was a better option, all things considered. "I waited to see who picked it up, but there was a fight a couple of alleys over. Big ruckus. Cops everywhere, so I ran. I didn't see what happened to the bag, but when I went back later, it was gone. The cops were still there," I added under my breath.

"And yet you aren't in jail." Val's smooth cheeks grew lined with irritation. "Imagine my surprise."

"Serendipity." I eased a little closer to the window under the pretense of adjusting the curtains. "Some lawyer took a shining to me, that's all."

"Some lawyer?" The shorter of the two daughters snorted, biceps bulging as she folded her arms. "Benedict Chase isn't just some lawyer, kid."

Kid. My heart-rate dropped and my blood chilled. The cold gathered around my eyes until my sinuses felt full and heavy, my forehead stiff. Val might pose a problem, but her daughters could be easily disposed of if the scary mojo got offended. I didn't look at her directly but the timbre of my voice dropped significantly as I said, "Val, we have rules."

The hyena queen's upper lip curled, but she snapped, "Go wait in the hall," and the daughters obeyed without a single word. The short one gave me a dirty look, though I didn't care. Her mother just saved her damn life.

Val folded her arms over her chest and took a stalking step toward me once the door shut behind them. "She's right. Benedict Chase is not someone I want sniffing around my ... employees."

"Good thing I don't work for you." It came out more flippantly than I intended, by the way her expression darkened.

Layla Nash

I held up my hands, though my eyes burned with cold and fury. It would take hours before the mojo settled back down. "It was nothing. He wanted to be a white knight, I let him."

"He's dangerous for us." It wasn't exactly fear that gathered in the lines around her mouth, but it was just short of that. "His kind are trouble. They're lions, Eloise. They do not tolerate my kind, or yours."

I snorted and pinched the bridge of my nose, even though my hands trembled. Benedict fucking Chase. Of course. I should have looked at the business card. "He's not in the picture, as I said. And I don't know what to tell you about the money, Val. I'm sorry they didn't bring Lacey to the drop-off point. Did they try to call?"

Her mouth twisted and she flicked at the window curtains. "I have heard nothing from my daughter." She faced me again, expression composed to indifference once more. As if her daughter hadn't been kidnapped. "And here is my problem, Eloise. I paid ten thousand dollars to get my daughter back. You lost the money. Now I have neither ten thousand dollars, nor my daughter."

My heart dropped. "I didn't lose the money, Val. I left it *exactly* —"

"You had the money, the money disappeared, and no one saw where it went. Not even you." Her tawny skin wrinkled, almost cracked, as her teeth bared. "So forgive me for not taking the word of a petty criminal."

"I'm a damn good criminal," I shot back, too unnerved by her accusation to let it pass without challenge. If she thought I'd stolen her money and condemned Lacey to death, I was totally fucked. "Or you wouldn't claim me as an employee, would you? I did what you told me to do, Val. Maybe the wolves took it. Or the kidnappers aren't playing by the rules. How the fuck do I know?"

"Very well." She stalked closer and I stood my ground, though my heart plummeted. Her fingers, wizened and wrinkled and with thick nails twice as long as mine, pressed just below the hollow of my throat. "You get one more chance, little gorgon. Find my money, or find my daughter. If you don't, I own you until you repay the debt."

The cold rage prickled through my temples and out my eyes, and I debated testing out the mojo. I stared at her nose, close enough to her eyes that sweat broke out on her upper lip. "I'm not going to —"

"You have two days." She took a step back, eying me from head to toe. Her broad shoulders squared and she looked more like an aged prize fighter than someone's granny. "Fix it."

Whatever objection I might have offered died in my throat as she walked out. I massaged my temples to try to fix the magic that collected around my eyes. Not now. Really not the time. I'd have a fucking migraine for a week at this rate.

I grabbed my phone and checked to make sure the hall was clear. Lacey would have the answers. It seemed like a good idea at the time, scamming her mother out of seed money so Lacey and her boyfriend could start over in Europe, far away from hyena politics, but me ending up a wage slave to the hyena queen was not part of the plan. Lacey would have to call her mother and explain. Return the money or show proof of life. Something.

I couldn't be indebted to the hyena queen. Valentina Szdoka was almost as ruthless as the Chase brothers. I pinched the bridge of my nose. The CEO, Logan, was the worst, but his lawyer brother wasn't far behind. They were legendary among the city shifters for being cold-blood negotiators and businessmen, unfeeling as they dismantled and sold and bought and traded. I fished the business card out of the jeans in the shopping bag, and almost threw it out the window. Benedict Chase.

But the memory of his smile comforted me as I headed out into the night to call Lacey. If what Val threatened came to pass, I would need a hell of a lawyer to extricate myself from her clutches. A lawyer who could turn into a lion might be worth the exorbitant retainer, particularly since the hyena queen seemed disconcerted by him already.

I wondered if he offered a payment plan.

chapter 5

None of Val's daughters hung around outside that I could
find, and none of her sons loitered at the corner. I kept my
head down and half-jogged a couple of blocks until I found a
working pay phone. Lacey's was one of two numbers I knew
by heart.

After a couple of rings, my heart thudded against my chest
loud enough I feared Val might hear and track me down again
for being chicken-shit. She didn't tolerate cowards, but she put
up with liars. So I lied about being a coward.

I concentrated on keeping my breathing even and calm. In
through the nose, out through the mouth. Two days. Plenty
of time.

"Hello?" Her voice reached me, slow and sluggish. "Who
is this?"

"Lacey? What the hell is going on?"

"Ellie? Where are you?"

"Where am I?" I slapped my forehead, glancing over my shoulder as something moved in the alley. "Lacey, what happened? Why haven't you called your mother? The money's gone and she's blaming me."

"Something went wrong." She sounded distant, her voice tinny. Confused. Maybe afraid. "I don't know where I am. It's dark. Smells wrong. And Cal isn't —" The words broke off, muffled. Static. Then loud banging.

"Lacey," I said, dread growing in my stomach. It was just a simple con. A quick scam. Easy. Nothing should have gone wrong.

"Someone else was there," she whispered. "I think they hurt Cal. Please, El — help me. Please. You have to help —"

The line cut off.

I stared at the pay phone, dropped the handset. Turned in a circle to search the night. Lacey. She was really in trouble. My fingers shook as I dialed her number again. Straight to voicemail.

"Oh no," I said, and I reached out to balance against the phone box. Kept repeating it over and over, because nothing else made sense. I fumbled my cell phone and nearly dropped it, searching the contacts for a number. Cal. Maybe Cal knew what the fuck was going on.

His phone rang and rang, but eventually a cold voice answered. "What?"

"Is C-cal there?"

"Who's asking?"

"A friend of Lacey's. She's worried about him, can't —"

"That *bitch*." The next words disappeared in a snarl, only getting back to coherent after I cursed at the phone. The speaker's voice dripped derision. "That stupid whore tricked him, and some of her bitch friends jumped him. He's in a coma. He's not getting better, they shot him with something before they broke every bone in his body. So Lacey can go fuck herself, because as soon as we find her, she's dead."

I opened my mouth, words caught in my throat, but that line went dead, too. I closed my eyes. Cal in a coma, Lacey somewhere dark. And the hyenas and jackals on a collision course to war. A real war. And if their battles spilled into other territory, the rest of the shifters would be drawn in. Humans as collateral damage. It would be a bloodbath.

I left the phone off the hook as I trudged away, mind spinning and clicking along too slowly to match my feet. My head pounded. I kept shaking it but it didn't help. I took my hair out of the bun, thinking the tension maybe contributed, but I knew it was the mojo and rage and fear that had my vision sparking with floating white dots. Bad sign, that.

The walk back to the hotel took an eternity. If I told Val what happened, she'd kill me for helping her daughter scam her. Or she might kill me for getting her daughter for-real kidnapped. Or the jackals would kill me for contributing to Cal's beating and coma. Or maybe Benedict Chase would kill me for stealing his wallet.

My fingers felt numb as I pressed them against my eyes. The streets passed in a blur until I staggered in the rear entrance to the crappy hotel, wanting another shower. A hot shower. Maybe if I cranked the tap all the way, it would approach hot. And sleep. I couldn't think of ways to save Lacey and fix Cal on two hours of sleep over the last three days. It made me sloppy. I hated sloppy.

Layla Nash

The door to my room opened without the key, and I frowned. It was still on the counter in the bathroom where I dropped it. I shook my head and walked in, leaning back against the door after it closed, and froze.

Benedict Chase, wearing the same suit and looking like a tall bit of delicious, stood near the window. His frown turned thoughtful, then concerned. "Eloise, are you okay? You look a bit — peaked."

A laugh escaped before I could bite it back, and my legs gave out. I slid to the floor, still laughing. Damn the luck.

chapter 6

The hotel was worse than he imagined, but a little better than Benedict feared. The front desk confirmed that a room was rented in his name; the clerk even gave him the number. He waited across the street in a coffee shop, sipping a cappuccino as he watched the moderate foot traffic through the lobby. Mostly people who looked like they only needed a room by the hour. He debated confronting her in the hotel, and had just made up his mind to do so when a pair of dark sedans rolled up.

Benedict kept his seat. There weren't many people in the city who went out and about in armored cars, and very few of them had any reason to be in that part of town for legitimate business. His eyebrows climbed to his hairline when he saw the older woman who got out of the lead car, followed by two shorter but stockier women. Valentina Szdoka.

He drummed his fingers on the table. What were the hyenas doing in this part of the city? Technically this territory belonged to one of the wolf packs, though they allowed the other predators to transit unchallenged during business hours. The queen of the hyenas came dangerously close to violating half a dozen treaties.

Benedict snapped a few photos of the hyenas with his phone, just in case he needed to bring it up with Logan later, and debated how long to wait before going after Eloise. The hotel floorplan gave him an idea of where her room was, and as he stared at the window, the curtains moved. Her face, pale and uncertain by the streetlight, called to him. She wasn't happy. Looked afraid or at least unhappy and concerned. His lion grumbled, started to pace in the back of his head. His girl needed help. Needed him.

He tried to shake off the feeling that she was his — they'd had lunch together, that was it. And he'd bailed her out of jail. It was hardly the start of a solid relationship.

He answered the ringing phone without thinking. "Yeah?"

"How goes the stakeout?"

"Trouble," he said, never taking his eyes off that window. His chest tightened as he saw Val's hard-eyed face near the curtain. But he didn't tell Edgar that. The moment Edgar knew the hyenas were involved, he'd gather the storm troopers and clear the area. Send a message. He wouldn't tolerate them long enough to find out why Val Szdoka visited Eloise in a shitty hotel the same day he bailed her out of jail. And Benedict knew that running off Val meant Eloise would disappear as well. "But nothing I can't handle."

Edgar sighed. "You wouldn't tell me if it were bad, would you?"

"Probably not." Benedict managed to sound cheerful as Val and her troop of daughters exited the hotel, argued briefly, then got into their cars and sped away. He got up and headed for the hotel lobby. "So don't worry about it."

"Put a chain on your wallet, shithead."

"Thanks, dick." Benedict hung up and shook his head, avoiding the reception desk to take the stairs up to the second floor.

The door to her room stood open a crack, and Benedict took a deep breath. He eased inside, listening for any movement or breathing or ambushes. Nothing. He returned the door to its partially-open state and searched the room for any indication of what happened. The hyenas left through the front, but Eloise must have escaped out the back before he managed to get up the stairs. She was certainly quick on her feet.

Her clothes filled a bag in the corner, but it was a cheap paper shopping bag from a thrift store. His nose wrinkled. She could have at least used his credit cards to buy good stuff. New stuff. Something soft and plush against her skin. Lingerie, maybe. Benedict examined the bathroom, though he didn't dare touch anything — suspicious mildew covered most of the tile and all of the shower, and though a hint of her scent lingered in the air, he felt better waiting on the stained carpet in the main room.

He didn't wait long. He heard her coming from the stairs, the uneven tread of her feet matched by raspy breathing. His heart started to pound — she was upset. Maybe in trouble. Maybe hurt. His lion growled. She leaned through the door and shut it, eyes half-closed, but went still when she finally noticed him near the window. He cleared his throat and hoped he didn't sound like a fussy aunt. "Are you okay? You look a bit peaked."

She laughed at him, laughed hard enough she fell down, and he frowned down at her in consternation. Well, that was unexpected. The laugh turned almost watery, and Benedict moved slowly to help her stand. "What's wrong with you?"

"I'm tired," she said, eyes dazed as she looked around. For once, she didn't avert her gaze or hide her face, and he loved it. Loved every line and curve of her face, the sensuous bow of her lips, the long dark eyelashes that brushed her cheeks as she blinked slow and often. Silver pooled and sparked in her eyes, mesmerizing, and his lion purred. Stretched and wanted to rub himself all over her to mark her. Whatever kind of non-human she was, it was his kind.

Benedict helped her stagger to the mattress, though he flinched as she stretched out on the comforter. No telling what types of evidence decorated the ancient, somewhat waxy fabric. But Eloise had no similar reservations, though she clapped her hands over her face. "What are you doing here?"

He took a breath and she sat bolt upright, eyes wide and throwing sparks. "Are the cops here? Are they coming? Did you turn me in?"

He held up his hands to stem the flow of questions, laughing a little as he lowered himself into the least objectionable chair at the foot of the bed. "Whoa there. No cops. I didn't report the cards stolen, if that's what you're worried about."

She exhaled a gust of worry and some of the tension faded from her expression. She flopped back onto the mattress, once more covering her face until her words came out muffled. "I'm sorry I took your wallet."

He laughed, leaning forward enough to catch hold of her ankle, thin and delicate in his hand. "No you're not."

A hint of a chuckle, following by a groan. "I am, really I am. I don't know why I do it sometimes. It just happens."

"That's usually what my brother says when I bail him out of jail, so at least this is something I've heard before."

She cracked an eye open and lifted her head to give him a jaundiced look. "I'm trying to apologize."

"Rather than give me platitudes," he said, squeezing her leg. "Why don't you tell me what's going on?"

"I can't." Her legs moved a little, not quite kicking him away, but uneasy. He didn't release her. The lion wanted her to get used to his touch. She sighed and quieted. "You're a lawyer."

"See, most of the time when people hear I'm a lawyer, they tell me everything I never wanted to know about them." He watched the rise and fall of her chest, glad her breathing steadied and grew smoother, less panicked. At least she felt safe enough to take a damn submissive posture, sprawled out on her back with her soft underbelly exposed. "So let's start with something easy. What are you, exactly?"

"I'm tired," she said again, barely more than a breath.

"You know what I mean." Most lions had limited patience.

She went up on one elbow to study him, as if measuring his intentions. "I'm not a shifter."

"I didn't ask what you aren't, Eloise," he said, trying to find more patience when the lion only wanted to jump on the bed and curl up with her. On top of her. Cuddle her close until she smelled like him and those fucking hyenas left her alone. His lip curled at the thought of those fucking scavengers trying to strong arm his Eloise into anything.

"Big scary lion," she said with a yawn. She sat up enough to pull off her hooded sweatshirt, and though his heart jumped in anticipation, she wore a t-shirt underneath. It stretched across her small chest as she wormed around and kicked the covers back. "It's late. I'm tired and cold and just got some bad news about a friend of mine."

"Eloise..." His hands flexed on his knees. He wanted to pick her up and take her some place a lot nicer than this dump. A hotel with clean sheets and bathrooms that didn't look like a mad scientist's lab experiment.

Her eyes glowed in the half-light as she sat and eased to the edge of the mattress. Benedict sat back, almost unable to breathe. Beautiful. Her skin almost vibrated as she eased close enough that his hands settled on her waist, and she stood between his knees. Her head tilted to the side as she studied his mouth, the long dark ropes of her hair spilling down her back and across his hands.

"Benedict," she murmured, and it shot through his brain like electric current. Her knuckles brushed his cheek, and her eyes fixed his with a soul-searching intensity. "Dear Benedict. Are you also tired?"

"I could — could sleep," he said, making his voice deeper for no reason that he could understand. All he could see was her eyes, quicksilver as mercury, and the rose tint of her lips. The flush climbing her cheeks. Something wasn't quite right, but he couldn't remember what that was when she touched him.

She smiled, small white teeth even and nonthreatening. "Are you also cold, dear Benedict?"

He was. Suddenly he was cold enough to want to crawl into that bed and lay with her, skin to skin. Feel the warmth of her tangled up in his limbs. Eloise's head tilted to the side, a decidedly nonhuman gesture, and it nearly jolted him awake. He felt, in a sudden rush, hunted. As if he were prey. As if she

Chasing Trouble

were a scary, scary predator with the cunning to manipulate a lion into walking willingly into her trap.

And then her lips drifted across his and all that faded away to nonsense. He was a lion, after all. King of the jungle. Master of all animals. Fiercest of predators, as long as you didn't count the polar bears. Those motherfuckers were crazy.

"No, no, dear Benedict," she murmured, and then her weight balanced on his knees, her palms smoothing down his chest as she loosened his tie. She kissed his jaw, near his ear, and nibbled on his earlobe. "No thinking any other thoughts. Not now. Just think of me."

"Just Eloise," he said, and his grip tightened on her sides. Easy enough, when she was warm and wiggly in his lap. He smiled, sat back, and tried to remember why it might have been a bad idea. Nothing came to mind, particularly after she took off her t-shirt.

chapter 7

It was not my finest moment. I'd slept with guys for less, of course, but still. Benedict was a nice guy. He might be a lawyer and a lion and an overall dick to pretty much everyone in the world, but he'd been nice to me. The only way to save his life was to get him to stop asking questions about my business with Val. And the fastest way to get a guy to stop asking questions was to give him something to do with his mouth.

At least he was handsome. And a lot fucking stronger than I bargained for, as his arms tightened around me and he pressed his face between my breasts. I kept fiddling with his shirt and tie, wishing I'd gotten stretchy jeans as the denim dug into my waist. Definitely going on a diet. If I lived through the week.

I pushed the thought away. Put away the concern for Lacey and the uneasiness over what could have broken all of Cal's bones, and I even tried to ignore the stark raving terror of dealing with Val. I'd used the scary mojo on Benedict when

I first walked in and he hadn't flinched. Hadn't even noticed, really, because he still tried to use his lawyer voice to make me admit what I was. Everyone feared me, whether I wanted them to or not. And yet he stood there, unwavering, as I stared at him. Unbelievable.

His mischievous left hand slid down the small of my back and into my jeans, and I jumped forward. He laughed, leaving a trail of searing kisses across my chest and over my bra. "Ticklish, are you?"

"No," I said under my breath, but that was another one of my favorite lies. I wasn't ticklish like I wasn't a coward. My head tilted back as he squeezed my butt, and I revised my plans. Sleeping with him would be worth it, even if it cost me an hour. I slid my hand down between us, over the front of his trousers, and blinked. Maybe two hours. Fuck it, maybe I'd stay the whole night. Finding a man who wasn't immediately dick-droopingly terrified of me was pretty rare.

Finding one who also had an enormous hard-on and hands like a Swedish masseur was even rarer.

I rocked my hips to his and tore at his shirt, the buttons flying across the room. The mojo wanted him too, and I didn't think I could have stopped for any amount of money in the world. "Clothes. Off."

He grumbled something in his chest and stood, taking me with him until I floated, legs wrapped around his waist. Benedict smiled, looking all love-drunk and adorable, and he kissed me. It started sweet, like him, then deepened until I drowned, until the cold melted out of my eyes and fire ignited instead, until molten lava cascaded through my veins and all of me caught fire. My fingers ran up the back of his neck and into his hair, working at his scalp to keep his face close to mine.

Benedict dropped me on the bed and I bounced, trying to take a deep breath as he loomed over me. "Normally," he said, voice deep and rough. "I like to take my time."

I sat up and pulled at his belt, felt the fire consuming me from the inside out. "Don't make me wait."

He laughed, but it was half-purr, and he kissed between my breasts as he tugged on the button of my jeans. Fumbling clothes off took too much time but eventually our shoes and pants were off and his weight settled against me. He kissed my cheek, my jaw, bit at my earlobe, and I wiggled, hands sliding to his lower back. Benedict grumbled, fingers bold at my hip. "Did you know your underwear is inside out?"

My cheeks heated and I bit him back, taking his lower lip in my teeth before saying, "Is that really all you noticed?"

"Well," he said. His knee nudged between my thighs after he stripped off the offending garment, and his fingers traced a fiery trail down my hip and over my stomach, sliding down and over the aching flesh where desire gathered. I sighed and moved my hips, lifting to facilitate as he stroked and probed and gently explored territory no one had been brave enough to dare in years. "I may have sensed something else."

I knew it was the mojo working on us both. I knew it. I still wanted him, still pulled him on top of me until that massive cock nudged at my body and eased inside. He looked drunk or drugged, gaze fuzzy and heated as he kissed me. But even with the lust and burning magic between us, he held himself above me, careful to rock back and forth until my muscles relaxed and he slid deeper. There was none of the forceful thrusting or fucking or rutting that I expected from the lion, only a gentle taking, possessing. Asking.

My back arched as his stomach rested against mine and it was too much, too full, with a deep ache. His mouth trailed down my throat. "Are you okay?"

"Too much," I whispered, running my hands up his cheeks to seize his hair. "I love it but it's too much."

He kissed me, tongue lazily exploring my mouth as he eased back and I could breathe. His body slipped from mine and he squeezed my hip. "Get on top of me, baby."

Benedict lay on his back, muscles tense, and helped me slide onto his chest. He held himself still and guided me back until he entered me and I tensed, sighing with the unbelievable heat of his body. He countered the fire in my chest from the mojo, the angry gorgon blood running in my veins, and Benedict kneaded my ass to pull me down on his cock. "A little more, baby."

I lay full-length on him, head on his shoulder, and rocked until I felt complete. Full and complete and connected to him in a way I hadn't ever felt before. Ever. I moaned as he kept squeezing my ass and hips and thighs, pulling my knees to either side of his hips so I could brace and begin a leisurely ride.

He murmured in my ear, kissing me and squeezing my breasts and grasping at where my thighs sloped up to my butt, but he let me set the pace. The fire swirled up inside me and my muscles seized up, clamping down on him, and Benedict groaned, hips lifting to meet me for the first time in a sudden thrust. I cried out as stars sparked in my eyes and I couldn't move, almost paralyzed as pleasure rolled through me, wave after wave, and still he moved, thrusting steadily when I remained still.

Benedict's arms tightened around me, kept my breasts flattened against his chest as he moved with more urgency, more force, and another orgasm steamrolled through me. He growled in my ear and went rigid, jerking underneath me as the hot rush of his release flooded my insides. My eyes closed as I rested my head on his chest, listening to his racing heart. A fine sheen of sweat covered both of us; a drop beaded on my temple, rolled down my cheek and dropped to his chest.

He petted my back from shoulders to ass, over and over in a soft stroke that had me stretch and settle against him. Benedict kissed my forehead, exhaling in a gust as he reached for the sheet to cover us both. Something like a purr rumbled through him, turned into a snore.

I only meant to close my eyes for a moment to enjoy the afterglow and the strength of his arms around me, but the next time I lifted my head, the battered alarm clock on the side table said it was almost one a.m. With the mojo faded along with the rage and fire, reality set in. I had two days, probably less, to find Lacey and figure out who stole the money. I couldn't waste any more time canoodling with Benedict Chase.

He still slept, a snore rattling in his throat, and smacked his lips as I untangled myself and slid to the end of the bed. I got dressed after cleaning up as best I could — I didn't dare another shower, either from fear of waking him up or catching something toxic from that bathroom. I gathered his clothes and shoes and phone, and stuffed them into my shopping bag, looking back regretfully at where he still slept. If he chased after me, Val would kill him. She would figure out a way to kill the lion.

The thought haunted me as I slid out of the room and then out of the hotel, heading to a familiar bar a few blocks away. Calling in a favor from the owners of O'Shea's wasn't the way I would have liked to end the night, but it beat trying to go home. Doubtless the Chase brothers would be able to track me there. I needed to go to ground, and if any of the packs had a problem with Val using their territory for the ransom drop, Rafe would have heard about it.

I slid into O'Shea's and through a crowd of what looked like frat boys. I kept my eyes down but they still cleared a path, most looking at me and then moving uneasily away. Too much of the scary stuff still floating around me. I made a beeline for the bar, where Rafe pulled pints and Ruby argued with a couple of girls with clearly fake IDs. Rafe's dark, raven-wing eyebrows rose as he looked at me. "Well. Look what the cat dragged in."

My cheeks burned but I slid onto the bar stool without wincing too much. My lady parts would definitely remember Benedict Chase for a while. I rested my elbows on the bar. "I need a drink, but I need some information more."

He leaned to consider the paper bag of clothes I left by the end of the bar. "That's it?"

"Maybe a place to sleep it off tonight. If you don't mind."

"Hmm." He put a beer in front of me, then rested his elbows on the smooth wood of the bar. "What do you need to know?"

"Lacey Szdoka was kidnapped night before last, and last night someone stole the ransom money but didn't deliver the girl. Do you know who's got her?"

Rafe let out a low whistle, stepping back as if to get distance from just a hint of the hyena band's troubles. "Shit. Who'd be stupid enough to take one of Val's kids?"

I squirmed a little, trying to keep the door in the corner of my eye. Just in case Benedict Chase was psychic, too, and knew where I went. "That's what I'm trying to find out. The ransom drop happened about six blocks west of here, in the alley behind Aaron's Chili Bowl."

He glanced over at Ruby, then shook his head as he considered me. "That's not our turf, but the SilverLine Pack might know if anything funny happened. Have you dealt with Miles and his guys before?"

I pinched the bridge of my nose as the migraine returned with a throbbing agony. Miles Evershaw and his band of merry men. I sighed. "Not recently. Most wolves don't like me."

"We'll send someone with you." Rafe concentrated on slicing a few limes and tossing them into the mixed drinks for a few frat boys farther down the bar. "But tell me, why is this your problem, Eloise?"

"Val is making it my problem," I said, closing my eyes as I drank and the cool alcohol extinguished some of the brimstone still percolating in my guts. "I dropped the ransom and she thinks I stole it instead."

"Did you?" Ruby asked, frowning as she took up real estate next to her brother.

Offended, I put a hand to my chest and sat back. "Moi? How dare you."

Her only response was to raise one of her slightly less-bushy eyebrows.

I winked and finished the beer. "Of course I didn't. I know better than to steal from Val Szdoka."

"What about from Benedict Chase?"

I choked on the beer, almost snorted it out my nose, and spent the next minute coughing and hacking and trying to breathe. When I finished, eyes watering as I struggled to inhale, Ruby didn't look away from me as she gestured at the bag. "Because some of his stuff is in that bag, and if I'm not mistaken, some of his ... stuff is in you, too."

"Holy shit, Ruby," her brother said under his breath, looking a little embarrassed on my behalf. "Mind your fucking business."

"She wants to shelter in our den, it's my business who she's fucking and who she's fucking over." Ruby pointed a crimson talon in my face. "Look at me, kid."

I ground my teeth but did as she said, knowing that the quicksilver in my eyes would throw her into the line of liquor bottles behind her. Rafe took a step back but Ruby remained leaning over the bar, unmoved and unimpressed. "Here's the thing, chickie pie. Our pack is officially unofficially connected to the Chases. So I'm going to ask, on behalf of Logan Chase and his mate Natalia Spencer, what is the nature of your relationship with Benedict Chase?"

The words caught in my throat as I stared at her, wondering why the mojo didn't work on Ruby O'Shea. She waited. When I managed to speak, though, my voice came out smaller than I intended. "He helped me. I ... thanked him. That's it."

Her eyes narrowed, dark and deep. "Your word that your relationship with Benedict is not at the direction of or for the benefit of Valentina Szdoka?"

"It's not." I cleared my throat and squared my shoulders. Time to be a big girl and a scary gorgon. "I'm trying to protect him from her. She did not like that he helped me."

Ruby made a disgruntled noise, then shoved off the bar and upright once more, glancing at her watch. "Okay. Get your ass upstairs and shower. Tomorrow morning you're going to mop the floors in here and help me drag stock up from the basement, and I'll have someone take you over to Miles."

Rafe shook his head and help up his hands. "Sorry, El. I would have let you stay for free, but everyone knows Ruby's meaner than I am."

"No shit." I got to my feet, feeling wobbly. "What am I going to have to pay Miles to get any info?"

"That's between you and Miles." Ruby snapped her fingers at one of her pack minions and gave directions to contact the other pack and start arranging the complex meeting arrangements. "So best figure that out yourself. It won't be cheap."

I sighed and dragged towards the stairs, just past the office they shared. "Thank you, Ruby. Please don't tell anyone about Benedict. It's not something I want spread around."

"Then get in the fucking shower," she said under her breath. "We have noses, you idiot. And you're welcome. Get some sleep, you look like hell fucked over."

"Go fuck yourself," I said under my breath, though my face burned as I climbed the stairs to their guest quarters. That was the worst part about working with shifters — they knew more about you than you could ever know about them. Not that I wanted to know when someone was in heat.

At least their shower had scalding hot water and fluffy towels and neutral shampoo and no mildew or creepy stuff on the floor. I stood under the stream of water and tried to force the tension from my shoulders. Mopping floors would be worth it just for the shower. Everything else could wait until tomorrow.

chapter 8

He dreamed of her. And when he woke up, the bed was empty. Not even the pillow retained an indent, and he wondered if she'd used some sort of spell on him. Maybe she was a witch, with those crazy damn eyes.

Benedict groaned as he sat up and looked at the clock, scrubbing a hand over his face. He needed to shave before he started to look like Logan. He looked around for his clothes and shoes and phone, and found nothing. Abso-fucking-lutely nothing. Anger boiled up in his gut as he made a quick tour of the room, then put his fist through the wall. Unbelievable. She took everything. Every scrap of clothing. His wallet — *again*. No note, no explanation, nothing. Just slipped out like she'd never been there. Like they hadn't slept together.

The memory of her warm body encasing his, welcoming him, moving over him contradicted the disregard of her disappearing act, and Benedict sat on the bed, head in his hands. It didn't make sense. She returned from arguing with the hyenas, slept with him, then disappeared again. If she needed help, she would have stayed around. If Szdoka wanted to trap or kill him, he'd be dead. Finished.

He picked up the cheap phone on the bedside table, praying it worked, and was both relieved and resentful when it did. He dialed Edgar's cell phone, pinching the bridge of his nose to keep a headache at bay. That goddamn girl. His lion grumbled and growled as the phone rang, wanting to track her down. She carried his scent, she was his. She needed to be with him.

Edgar's voice was rusty with sleep. "What the fuck do you want?"

"Pick me up."

A groan, then a sigh. "What happened?"

"Don't want to talk about it. I'm at the hotel. Room 202. Bring a go bag up."

"Why?"

Benedict didn't have to see his brother's face to know a slow smile crept over his expression. He gritted his teeth and covered his eyes. "Give me a break."

"I'm not getting out of bed until you tell me why you need the go bag."

"She took my clothes." Each syllable sent him further and further into fury and grief. Why had she left? "Get over here."

A chuckle, but at least it sounded like Edgar moved. "And how did she get all your clothes, big guy?"

"Fuck. Off." But he didn't hang up. Benedict stared at the stained carpet, toes curling up from touching it. Christ, he needed a shower. Or twenty. And industrial strength soap and steel wool.

"Slept with her, didn't you." It was one of Edgar's specialties, asking a question as if it weren't.

"Yeah." He sighed. "Just get here, will you?"

"Give me thirty minutes." Edgar yawned, words lost in the grumble, then followed up with, "Your girl is quite a cipher, brother. See you in a bit."

The line went dead and Benedict stared at the receiver in his hands. Cipher wasn't quite the word for it. Mysterious, intoxicating, intriguing, annoying as hell... Those all worked.

It took Edgar forty minutes. Benedict, still naked, paced a short circuit through the small, dingy room, throwing the door open when he heard a knock. He took the go bag and almost shut the door in his brother's face based just on Edgar's grin.

Edgar grimaced as he shut and locked the door, looking around the room with raised eyebrows. "Jesus, Benedict. This is where you take your girl for a night of fun?"

"Not my idea. I would have taken her to the Plaza but we didn't get a chance to — talk about it first." He dug through the go bag and found the extra clothes, started dressing so he could get home and take a shower and figure out what the fuck he was going to do about Eloise.

"I'll bet you didn't." Edgar smirked, going to look out the window. He paused, sniffing at the fabric, then turned a shrewd gaze on his little brother. "Hyenas? Is she a hyena?"

"No." Benedict's clipped tone earned him a raised eyebrow look and folded arms. He cursed, holding his head to keep it from exploding with frustration. "She works for Val. Sort of. I think. Like I said, we didn't talk a lot."

Edgar made a thoughtful noise, continuing his tour of the room, and clasped his hands behind his back.

Chasing Trouble

Benedict knew they wouldn't leave until Edgar got to whatever point he wanted, and flopped back on the mattress in a deliberately submissive posture. Fuck it. He wanted breakfast more than he wanted to play dominance games. "Say what you've got to say, Ed. I'm tired and hungry and I want a shower."

"Not here." Edgar took another quick look around the room, then canted his head at the door. "Back at the office. I've got a few things to show you."

They left after Benedict returned the key to the front desk clerk, who raised her eyebrows but knew better than to say anything pointed. The ride to Edgar's office was silent, thank God, but Benedict's grinding teeth were loud enough to fill the car. Luckily very few people frequented the corporate offices on a Saturday, although the guard at the front desk offered only a bland smile and a wave. He was accustomed, at least, to the odd comings and goings of the Chase brothers. Benedict had just never been one of those odd footnotes, and he didn't particularly like it.

Edgar unlocked his office and canted his head at the attached bathroom as he headed for the desk. "Shower, if you want."

"Thanks, no." Benedict frowned, searching for a chair to sit in after the mess they'd made of everything the day before, and settled for perching on the arm of the couch they hadn't destroyed. "So what's up?"

"Do you think she's targeting you?"

Benedict blinked. "What?"

"She's not exactly your type, Benedict." Edgar didn't sit, instead only leaning his fists on the desk as he studied his younger brother. "And you've known her exactly two days, probably less. Is this deliberate?"

"I doubt it."

"Why?"

Benedict shook his head, thinking of that look on her face when he touched her, the way she laughed, the lightning in her eyes. Not even the best actresses could fake that. And the hints of fear when he asked about the hyenas, when she looked out the window. Something was very wrong, she was in trouble. "I just know it. She's in trouble, it has something to do with the hyenas."

Edgar studied him closely for long enough that Benedict's irritation grew and he almost took off his flip-flip to throw at him. Finally the security chief sat, though it sounded more like he collapsed. "Okay."

"Okay? Okay what?"

"Okay, if you choose her." Edgar frowned more, digging through a stack of folders on his desk. His office wasn't nearly as messy as Benedict's, but it wasn't as pristine as Logan's.

"What do you mean, if I choose her?" Benedict got up to pace, nervous energy making it too difficult to sit still. His lion wanted to be searching for her, to be out in the city finding her. Bringing her back. But he didn't want Edgar to start talking about choosing her, and the finality of his older brother's sigh made him nervous.

Edgar gave him a long-suffering look. "You slept with the chick in less than a day and you're about to jump out of your skin because you don't know where she is. She didn't smell like a lion, but is this a true mate thing?"

"I don't think so." Benedict didn't want to look at him, instead going back to the security monitors that recorded every entry and exit and stairwell in the entire building. "Regardless, she's gone. In the wind. I have no idea where she went."

"I might." Edgar held up a hand to cut him off when Benedict spun, ready to leave. "But first you're going to sit down and look at what I dug up. Here. This is her criminal record."

Benedict reluctantly took the file folder, opening it up and wincing at the mugshot. Not flattering lighting or a good angle for anyone, really, but she looked downright sickly. And young. Much, much younger than the woman he'd slept with. Eloise Deacon. He liked the sound of Eloise Chase a lot more, then dashed the thought from his mind and told the lion to shut the hell up. One day was not long enough to decide.

He paged through it, a few counts of petty larceny, evading arrest, drinking underage. Nothing earthshattering. He looked up at his brother. "So?"

"And this is her criminal record."

Another folder. Benedict's head tilted. Different mugshot, different name, same girl. Eloise Mulder. More small potatoes crimes, but a count of forgery and possession of stolen goods.

He opened his mouth to ask but Edgar held out more folders. "There are eight total. Eight different names, different mugshots, different series of crimes."

Benedict took them, juggling the papers and photos as he tried to reconcile the master criminal in the files with the girl who'd told him to take his clothes off. Who'd lain with her head on his chest and slept. He cleared his throat. "What is this — what does it mean?"

"Hard to say." Edgar sighed, leaning back in his fancy chair and looking out the full-length windows behind him. "Except she's probably not who you think she is, Ben. I'm sorry. By all accounts, she's not a violent criminal or a psychopath or anything, but she was arrested in the vicinity of some underground fight clubs. Several times. Too many times for it to be a coincidence."

"She's not a fighter." He shook his head, immediately rejecting the idea. "Not her."

"How do you —"

"No scars." Benedict looked at his brother, then back down at the records. "No scars anywhere, and she doesn't heal fast enough. She wouldn't survive in the fights. There has to be another reason she would be around there."

"Maybe you can ask Atticus."

Edgar said it so calmly, so casually, that Benedict answered before he even thought. "Maybe. I don't think Atticus pays attention to the crowd, though." And a heartbeat later, as the silence stretched, he sat back. Put the folders down to rub his temples. He needed some aspirin. Or a bottle of whisky. "How did you know?"

"That Atticus is a street fighter? I didn't, not for sure. Thank you for confirming it." Edgar's expression grew more severe as he sat up and made a few notes on a paper. "That's what he keeps getting arrested for?"

"Yes. He's going to stop." Benedict wanted to help Eloise, but Atticus was his little brother and he'd gone down a wrong path. He didn't want Edgar to bring the hammer down and ruin his life. "Let him figure it out."

"He's going to get killed. Or kill someone else." Edgar rubbed his jaw, beard rasping against his palm. "Then how are you going to explain that to Logan? And Mother?"

Benedict made a face, holding up his hands. "He's good. You talk to him, Ed, but don't get Logan involved. He'll break Atticus's legs to keep him from going, and that won't work. Not with baby brother."

The security chief sighed, then pointed at the file folders. "I'll think about what to do with Atticus, but that can wait. I'll just work the shit out of him until he's too tired to fight. What do you want to do with your girl?"

"She's not mine," Benedict said in a low voice. In the most recent mugshot, she looked tired. Exhausted and sad and beaten down. Like she was just waiting for the charges that kept her in jail.

"Do you want her to be?"

"I barely know her, as you pointed out."

Edgar glanced at his watch. "But if you want the time to get to know her, Ben, you need to make a decision. She's in with some awful people, not least of which is Val. And there's tension brewing around the hyenas with a couple other clans, but no one can really suss out why. If she's in the middle of it, early intervention will be necessary to keep her alive."

Benedict snorted. "You can't be —" but cut off when he saw Edgar's expression. "You seriously think she's in danger?"

Edgar gave him a long look, then shoved to his feet. "Leave the folders. I'll take you back to the house so you can clean up, then we'll meet Logan for dinner at O'Shea's."

"I don't want to put up with Ruby tonight, seriously." Benedict left the stack of paper on Edgar's desk. "And their food is terrible."

"Your girl stayed with Ruby and Rafe last night." His brother said it over his shoulder, as if it were nothing. "They know more about her, but they're not talking to me. Maybe if you ask with that stupid fucking lovesick look in your eyes, they'll spill."

Benedict almost tripped over himself following Edgar out of the office. "She stayed with them? Is she still there?"

"Yes, and no." Edgar shook his head as he punched the buttons on the elevator with more force than necessary. "But you know who we're dealing with, so get your shit together. Ruby is still irritated Logan claimed her best friend, so if you go in there and steal away one of her fences, it'll be even more."

"She's a fence?" Benedict ran a hand through his hair and stared at the blank elevator doors. "Great. At least she knows how to get rid of stuff."

By the look Edgar shot him, he wasn't impressed. Benedict couldn't quite hide his grin. The hunt was on.

chapter 9

I showered twice in the morning, before and then after mopping floors and doing way too much manual labor to cover a lumpy cot with noisy neighbors. But Ruby made me shower with her shampoo and soap, so I would smell like her when I talked to the other alpha. Something about marking me as under her protection. If the hulking bruiser driving me to the meeting didn't mark me as under her protection, I didn't think some shampoo would make much of a difference.

I braided my hair back, hoping it didn't cause any more trouble after my bodyguard, Lewis, sniffed near me and then sneezed. Damn wolves. My heart beat faster as we approached the alpha's compound, a large warehouse in the outskirts of the city. His territory encompassed a great deal of the downtown, but Miles Evershaw liked his space. Or so Ruby claimed, rolling her eyes. And from the tone of her voice, I wondered if there were more to that than she chose to reveal.

But when I started grinning, about to tease, Rafe made a sharp slicing motion across his throat and gave me the big eyes that meant to shut the fuck up. So I only smiled meekly and thanked Ruby for her help. And promptly undid it with a "holy fucking shit, what beanstalk did *you* fall out of?" when she introduced her nephew, Lewis.

He really was a giant, easily six foot five or taller, since I couldn't crane my neck enough to see the top of his head. And broad shouldered and gruff and more like a mountain than a man. Or wolf. The car ride was silent after I made a joke about rolling down the window and sticking my head out, and he gave me a sideways look that almost stopped my heart. I just put on my sunglasses, more to hide my eyes than anything else, since the fall sky was too cloudy for good sun.

I'd woken up a ball of nerves from not sleeping well, though my dreams were more of Benedict than of what awaited me at Val's hands if I failed. The thought of Lacey and Cal only made me more miserable as I tried to choke down break-fast. The memory of Benedict's hushed voice and murmured appreciation from the night before made me brave enough to face the alpha.

Miles Evershaw generally stuck with his own kind. The only reason he agreed to meet me was because Ruby asked, and the alphas of the two wolf packs that split the city gener-ally tried to stay on good terms. They had to, really, to balance the power of the lion pride, the hyenas, the jackals, the handful of bears roaming around, and other big cats. The wolves were more numerous but smaller, and relied on their packs to get shit done. Their organization meant they were more effective than any of the more democratic-minded shifters, and the alphas were all-powerful. Unfortunately, there weren't many female wolves left running around, so the boys were always on edge.

I chewed the inside of my cheek as Lewis slowed the car in the approach to the warehouse loading area, flashing his lights twice before sitting back to wait. I looked at him. "What's the hold up?"

"Security." He kept his hands on the steering wheel. "Don't make any sudden moves."

"Or what?"

"They'll shoot you."

"Oh." When I looked over, the corner of his mouth drew up in a smile and I couldn't tell if he were teasing or not. "It's not nice to make fun of people."

"I'm serious," he said, then used his chin to indicate the far corner of the building. "Don't move but you can see the light reflecting off the sniper up top."

"Fuck." I held my breath, trying to look inconspicuous and nonthreatening. My gorgon mojo might work on most of the pack, but it only took one wolf to rip out your throat.

Lewis received some signal I missed, because the car rolled into the lot and parked next to an enormous metal door. He got out, walked around the car, and opened my door, all the while scanning the surrounding area.

"Expecting an ambush?" I asked, trying to be funny.

"Usually." Lewis's hand landed heavy on the back of my neck, and he dragged me close enough to say under his breath, "Don't speak until spoken to. Be respectful. Don't try to be funny. And remember why you're here, and what you're willing to bargain. Don't make my aunt look stupid, got it?"

Layla Nash

I squeaked something that might have been acquiescence, because he nodded and walked toward the massive door. It rolled open and two hard-eyed shifters looked at us from inside. Lewis inclined his head slightly, hand tightening on my neck until I did the same. His voice rumbled out into the mid-day calm. "Lewis O'Shea and Eloise Deacon. Here to see your alpha, with thanks from the O'Shea family for his consideration."

The woman, looking like she was made of the same metal as the damn door, measured him from head to toe, then turned on her heel and strode into the building. "This way."

The male shifter remained where he was, and the door groaned shut behind us. I held my breath.

I didn't exhale until we reached the very interior of the warehouse, which seemed empty for a place of business. I made a mental note to ask Ruby what it was the SilverLine pack did to pay their bills, then thought better of it. I didn't like people prying into my business; based on the security, neither did Miles Evershaw.

The woman led us into a huge office with a massive desk, obsessively neat, as well as a six person conference table and a large sofa and two chairs. Coffee percolated off to the side. I desperately wanted some. The caffeine might not be as good as a shot of liquor to steel my nerves, but it would help. The alpha sat behind his desk, not acknowledging us as the woman disappeared out the door and shut it behind her. And so we waited.

I wanted to fidget. I desperately wanted to sit down, or fiddle with my watch, or check my phone. Lewis stood stone-still beside me, impassive and so damn silent I wondered if he'd actually just fallen asleep on his feet. Miles kept typing at his computer, then said, "My second will be here in a moment," and went back to his work.

Lewis said nothing, still waiting. I studied the SilverLine alpha, not daring take off my sunglasses lest I challenge him without meaning to. He wasn't quite as scary as I thought he'd be; though I'd heard plenty of stories about the bastard Miles Evershaw from the hyenas, I'd never seen the man in person. He was not much older than Benedict, maybe mid-30s, with the unlined skin of un-aging shifters. Broad shoulders, though I couldn't tell how tall he was from where he sat at the desk, but he didn't look bigger than meathead Lewis. Large hands, though, that dwarfed the computer mouse he used, snarling as he tried and failed to click something.

The door blew open behind us and a cheerful guy strode in, clapping Lewis on the back. "Hey mate. Been a while."

"Todd," Lewis said, shaking his hand.

The second-in-command for SilverLine studied me with an amused look on his face. "So you're what all the fuss is about? Little thing like you?"

Irritation rankled under my skin and I wanted to pull off the sunglasses, but as I tensed, Lewis's grip tightened on my neck. He still took a step back, though, as did the second. Miles looked up from his desk, frowning.

I cleared my throat, praying my voice stayed calm. "Thank you for agreeing to help. I appreciate —"

"I didn't agree to help you," the alpha said, power oozing from his voice and posture as he stood. "I agreed to hear you out."

"That is how we understood it, alpha," Lewis said, fingers digging into my neck, and I scowled at him.

Miles moved around to the front of his desk, leaning back against it as he studied me. "What's with the sunglasses?"

"Sensitive to light. Alpha," I said, shrugging a little to try to dislodge Lewis's grip.

"Lose them. I don't do business with someone if I haven't seen their eyes." And he waited, arms folded over his chest.

I chewed my lip but complied, folding the sunglasses and sticking them in my bag. I glanced near his face and then away, fidgeting with a loose string on my jeans. There weren't any windows in the office, and the walls slowly closed in around me.

Miles grunted, something like "Huh," then rubbed his chin. "What are you?"

So many rude men in that damn city. I bristled a little, the scary mojo bucking up more when I felt on edge. The upheaval of the last couple days put me in overdrive. "I'm not like you."

"Clearly." The alpha's eyes narrowed, and his second-in-command leaned on the edge of the desk, peering at me as well.

"I prefer not to say." It sounded ridiculous, small and weak in that testosterone-laden office of posturing and position and hierarchy. My preferences didn't matter a whole lot in that world. "I'm not a shifter of any kind, and I'm not a witch."

The wolves always worried about witches. Witches and hunters — that was all they cared about. Miles's impassive expression didn't thaw. "What do you want from me, girl?"

The scary mojo simmered and the cold gathered around my eyes. He didn't have to be a jerk about it. He already had all the power. No reason to be rude. Lewis took a step back, muttering something under his breath at me about keeping my shit together. I concentrated on Lacey, and Cal, and not being an indentured servant to Val Szdoka. "Two nights ago, one of the Szdoka girls was kidnapped. Thursday night, Val asked me to drop the ransom money near Aaron's Chili Bowl."

He made an irritated noise in his throat and the second's eyebrows rose. Lewis took another step back. Miles made a sharp gesture for me to continue, and I did, glancing between them for a long moment. "Cops chased me off before I could see who picked it up. When I went back, the money was gone, but the kidnappers didn't give Lacey back."

Todd, the second, tapped his chin. "So why are you here instead of the hyenas?"

I didn't want to admit my precarious position, but they already had all the power. They didn't have to help me at all, so I didn't really have anything to lose. "Val thinks it's some kind of scam I'm running on her. She wants her money or her daughter, or I'm dead."

Miles didn't speak for so long I wanted to break the silence, say or do something to alleviate the rising tension. Pressure built behind my eyes and I stared at his chest, concentrating on not going too far into panic and fear. That brought up the bad mojo just as quickly as being dismissed or called a kid.

The alpha frowned at me. "What do you want, then? Me to challenge the hyenas over them trespassing? Go to war with Szdoka over a botched ransom?"

"Fuck, no." I bit my lip as Todd's lips twitched, and my cheeks started to burn. Great. I cleared my throat and held up my hands. "That is, no, thank you. I just need information on who was on your territory that night so I can find the money. Or Lacey. I'd rather find Lacey. Someone bad has her and I want to get her back."

Layla Nash

Miles didn't move, his expression didn't change. He might as well have been a wax statue with a speaker attached. "Thursday night near Aaron's Chili Bowl. You left a bag of money and it disappeared, and now you want to know who took it."

"Yes." The silence stretched, so I added, "Please."

Todd, thin face definitely amused, fiddled with his phone. "Well, since you asked so nicely ..." I held my breath, not daring to hope.

The alpha studied me, head tilted. "Kitsune."

I blinked, startled into looking at him, and was caught. His alpha magic swirled up and his power rolled through the room, suffocating enough it sent Lewis reeling back almost to the door. I stood my ground, hands clenched at my sides, and a blizzard smacked into my eyes. My cheeks burned with cold, not embarrassment, and my hair grew heavier. Unbraided itself in jerky motions. I cursed, trying to break eye contact, but Miles refused to look away or let me go, even as the strain etched deep lines around his eyes. Beautiful gray eyes, he had, with dark lashes. My throat burned with the need to cry out, to scream my fury at the world, for the hate in my blood to escape along with the curses, but I held it in. Gripped the seam of my jeans and bore down, eyes narrowed. I managed to grind out a few words, "Release me. You have to release me."

Something crashed into me and I flew backwards, Todd's momentum taking us over the back of the chairs and onto the coffee table in front of the sofa. The maelstrom of power and challenge ebbed, faded away to nothing, and I groaned, pressed my hands to my eyes and fumbled for my sunglasses. Holy shit.

Todd, half on top of me, pushed himself up enough to look down at me. "What the hell was that?"

"I can't always control it," I said, not daring look near his face. Not wanting to think about how close I came to turning the SilverLine alpha, his second, and Ruby's favorite nephew into stone statues. "Thank you for — stopping it."

"You're welcome." His head tilted as he looked at me, an odd expression on his face. "You smell good."

"Oh. Um, thanks. That's Ruby's shampoo, so..." My hair lay loose and tangled under my shoulders, made it difficult to lift my head and see what happened to Lewis. Especially since Todd didn't seem inclined to let me up.

"No, it's something else." His head dipped and he pressed his nose against my hairline, near my ear, and inhaled so deeply his chest expanded against mine. "Huh. You smell like cloves, a little. Maybe. No, maybe cardamom." He did it again, and again, huffing and puffing against my hair and naming spices.

I tried to look back at where Lewis might be, bracing my hands on Todd's shoulders. "Could I, um, could I get up? This is a little weird."

"Sure." He didn't even blink, not embarrassed for a second as he jumped up, pulled me to my feet, and kept trying to smell me.

Irritated, I pushed him away. "Cut it out. It's her shampoo, I swear."

And found Miles still watching me, though his hair was a little ruffled. Lewis sat, face bloodless, near the door. Like his life had just flashed in front of his eyes. The SilverLine alpha's voice retained the exact same tone, measured and deliberate. "So not kitsune, I take it?"

"No." I cleared my throat and rubbed my upper arms, just wanting to be out of there. I'd wasted too much time already.

"If you know of any other clans or families on your territory Thursday night, I would appreciate if you could let me know."

"Appreciation doesn't help me." Miles straightened and walked around his desk, taking his seat once more. "I might know a few details that will help you, but I require something in return."

I braced myself for the worst and tried to ignore Todd standing next to me, trying to sniff me unobtrusively. I pushed him away. "Seriously, cut it out. I don't have any money, I can't —"

"I don't need money." The alpha drummed his fingers on the desk. "But I need whatever it is you just did. So. I tell you what I know, you owe me a favor."

"A favor?" Even I knew better. "What kind of favor?"

"Whatever kind of favor I need at the time I call it in." The alpha didn't blink. "Those are the terms, girl."

"That's crazy," I said, shaking my head. "Worst deal in history. Why would I ever agree to an open-ended favor?"

"Because otherwise you won't find out who took that ransom, and Mama Szdoka will kill you."

"But —"

"That's the deal."

Anger froze slowly over my heart and made it tougher to breathe. No wonder everyone hated this guy. But I didn't have a choice. If Miles told his pack not to help me, none of them would cross him. And I sure as hell couldn't go back to Aaron's, where we'd dropped the money, since Miles would put guards there to make sure the hyenas didn't return. This was my only option unless I took a loan from Bridger and Hanover, and I never wanted to do that again.

I swallowed hard, then nodded. "As long as the favor does not require harm to Ruby's pack, or the — the Chase pride, I'll agree."

Eyebrows arched, Miles leaned back in his chair. "The Chase brothers? How are you mixed up with the lions *and* the hyenas?"

"That's my business." I tried to look fierce without meeting his gaze.

The alpha studied me for another eternity, then nodded. "Very well. I will not ask you to do anything detrimental to the BloodMoon pack, nor will I ask you to do anything harmful to the Chase brothers. You owe me a favor of my choosing in the future, at a time of my choosing. Agreed?"

"Agreed." I held my breath.

Miles nodded, then handed me a slip of paper with an address and a phone number on it. "We chased two bears out of our territory that night, near enough Aaron's that they could have had something to do with it. The polar bear and the brown bear, I think. This is where you'll find them."

I swallowed hard, and a squeaked, "Bears?" escaped before I could bite it back.

For the first time, the alpha's facade cracked and a hint of a smile ghosted across his face. "I would offer backup but I'm guessing you can't afford it."

"No. Thank you." I retreated, the paper clutched in my hand. Fuck me running. I thought the hyenas were bad, and the jackals were worse, but no one fucked with the bears. No one.

Lewis needed my nudge to get up and get moving, but Todd helped with the door, getting in one last deep breath near me and muttering about "Turmeric?" before he stepped back, still in the office. Miles called, "I'll be in touch, Eloise," before the door shut.

My heart sank. I couldn't have described the route out of that warehouse if my life depended on it, nor could I remember a single detail from the drive through the city. The sky had darkened while we were inside, and a chill bit through me. My hands shook, almost tearing the paper.

Bears. A polar bear and a brown bear. If they had Lacey, she was as good as dead, or wishing she were. Dealing with the loan sharks would be less painful for me; at least I had a chance of surviving Bridger and Hanover. I put my face in my hands and concentrated on breathing. The day just couldn't get any worse.

chapter 10

For a Saturday night, O'Shea's wasn't particularly crowded. Benedict sat at the bar with his brothers and Natalia, Logan's mate, drowning his irritation and embarrassment in liquor. At least the food was better, since Natalia rolled her eyes and went into the kitchen to cook for everyone, despite the bartender's objections. Unfortunately, Benedict and the rest of the Chase clan had grown accustomed to a higher level of quality in their food since Natalia moved in with Logan a month earlier, so the regular pub food didn't quite cut it anymore.

Natalia sat on Logan's lap so he could nose around in her hair, though she didn't seem to even notice anymore as she concentrated on Benedict. "So where did you meet this girl?"

Edgar, leaning his elbows on the bar on the other side of Benedict, chuckled into his beer glass. "Jail."

She gave him a look and shook her finger at Benedict. "Really, Ben, you know better. She probably just wants your money."

Benedict grunted and poured himself another shot. It had been a terrible idea to come to O'Shea's. Ruby and Rafe weren't even there, but caught up in some pack business in the back office. So he hadn't learned anything useful about Eloise other than everyone else thought she was a gold digger.

Logan didn't look up from examining Natalia's ear. "Like you just want all my money."

She gave him a look that should have singed his eyebrows, and Benedict's forehead thunked against the bar. The very last thing in the world he wanted around him was a happy couple, flirting and giggling. Edgar laughed and slapped him on the back, leaning to say to Logan and his mate, "There's more."

"No there's not," Benedict said, voice muffled against the bar. "There certainly is not."

"She's mixed up with the hyenas."

A curse exploded out of Logan with enough force that Natalia looked startled, holding onto the bar as the lap she occupied became a great deal less stable. "Are you fucking kidding me, Benedict?"

Benedict held up his hands and forced himself to sit up. He held out his phone after pulling up the photos he took outside the hotel. "Val Szdoka and her family. No idea how they're connected, but they visited her at the hotel."

Logan took the phone and thumbed through the photos, his expression darkening. "No way. No, we're not having —"

"Eloise?" Natalia frowned at the screen, and Benedict's heart seized up. Edgar blinked. She glanced up, then pointed at the screen. "That girl is the one you're talking about? Eloise?"

"Yes," Benedict said slowly. He didn't dare look away from her lest he see Edgar and realize it was all a joke. "Do you know her?"

"Sort of." She looked a little uncomfortable as she shifted on Logan's lap, until he caught her waist and said something in her ear. Then she laughed and flushed, but stilled. She handed the phone back to Benedict. "She used to come into the soup kitchen where I volunteer. It's been a year since I've seen her there, I think, but she used to be a regular."

"The soup kitchen." It hurt to say, to think Eloise was so needy she had to seek charity for food. Someone hadn't cared for her enough.

"She was a tough kid." Natalia frowned, leaning back against Logan's chest. "A really tough kid. She stood her ground and even the mean guys there, the big guys who would try to bully the girls into tricking for them, even they left her alone. No one bugged her. I always wondered what it was. I mean, one time she was mad about something and I kind of got the chills, but I don't remember ever being afraid of her." Nat reached for her beer. "Still. Everyone else was."

"What else do you know about her?" Edgar asked when it became clear that Benedict couldn't speak. He held onto the bar for dear life, the lion raging that she'd been so mistreated. That some son of a bitch thought she would prostitute herself.

Natalia didn't seem to notice Benedict's turmoil. "She never talked much, but one of her good friends was chatty as hell and used to help me chop vegetables. It sounds like Eloise lost her mother when she was in her teens and spent a couple years in foster care, but it wasn't easy on her. Got bounced around a lot until she ended up in a group home. She hustled, though — I've never seen anyone work as hard as she did. I think some of that hustle was directed at illegal activities, but I never saw her hurt anyone. She was a nice enough kid, like I said, just a little odd."

Layla Nash

Benedict concentrated on his hands, the smooth glass between his fingers, the amber liquid sloshing around. A nice kid in foster care. No wonder she ran at the first opportunity. No wonder she looked for family with awful people like Val Szdoka. He braced himself to stand and stagger back outside to take a cab home for the night. "Great. If you don't mind, I'll —"

Ruby stormed out of the back office, face a thundercloud, and the entire bar immediately silenced. The pack members jumped to their feet or cowered, depending on rank, but none of them looked at her. Logan moved Natalia off his lap and ushered her behind the bar, out of harm's way, and looked at Ruby and her brother. "Is something wrong?"

"Fucking *Evershaw*." A snarl boiled up in her chest and Rafe wasn't far behind, eyes flashing gold and red.

Benedict wobbled to his feet, ready for a fight. If the SilverLine pack dared attack O'Shea's, he would stand with the O'Shea pack. Miles was just a dick.

Edgar tapped the bar near Ruby's elbow. "Do we need backup?"

"No," she ground out, and a light dusting of hair sprouted along her arms, disrupting the myriad tattoos she had.

Benedict blinked. He'd never seen *that* before. Before he could ask what happened, though, the front door blew open and a hulking beast of a man staggered in. Benedict recognized him from the bar, so knew the trouble wasn't due to Lewis's return, but then he saw who squeezed in the door next to him, and his heart stopped. Eloise.

She looked stunned, disoriented. Hurt. He lurched forward, a roar starting in his chest, but Edgar grabbed his arm and yanked him back. Ruby beat him across the bar to grab Eloise by the shoulders. "What the fuck happened? Why is Todd fucking Evershaw calling me, asking about you? *What did you do?*"

"Christ," Eloise said under her breath, lifting up a pair of mirrored sunglasses to rub her eyes. "Can the interrogation wait until I've had a dr—"

And then she spotted him, and all the color drained from her face. She ducked, tried to bolt, but Ruby still had her arm and then Logan did as well. He loomed over them and grabbed her, hauled her over to the bar as a chorus of growls erupted from the rest of the pack. Ruby snarled and turned her ire on Lewis, interrogating him as the man cowered as if she weren't a foot shorter than him.

But Benedict only cared about Eloise as she squeaked and cringed, and Logan's hands were on her, squeezing her arms, bruising her —

He launched forward and knocked his brother back, shoved his *alpha*, with a roar that silenced the bar for the second time that night. He kept Eloise behind him as he squared off with his older brother, ready to draw blood. "Don't touch her."

Logan's eyes narrowed, already flashing gold, and his shoulders grew as he flexed. "You challenging me, cub?"

"Don't touch her," was all Benedict could say. No other coherent thoughts could make it through the rage and fury. Eloise scared, and hurt, and trembling as she leaned against his back. "You *hurt* her."

"I did not and you know it." Logan's teeth showed, far pointier than any human's. "Back the fuck off, Benedict, or we will brawl right here."

Benedict couldn't move. Couldn't risk something happening to Eloise. So he waited, and the tension simmered. Ruby and her wolves gathered on the other side of the bar, giving them room in case the lions started throwing down. And then Natalia said very calmly, "Logan Chase, stop being a bully this instant."

He blinked. Logan did not, but his expression darkened. "Woman, now is not —"

"You scared that girl." Natalia edged herself between her mate and Benedict, shoving Benedict back a few steps to get room. "And you know it. Now cut it out and let's go home."

He grumbled and snarled, fighting it, but then Edgar flicked the back of Benedict's ear and he jumped. The spell broke. Tension eased. Eloise still trembled behind him, but Benedict could breathe.

chapter 11

Ruby was snarling from the moment we walked in, and I cringed back, thinking the other alpha called her about my little episode. I tried to hide behind Lewis, but he was absolutely worthless as she barreled around the corner and dragged me into the center of the room like I was a naughty kid. Before I could even really object, I looked up and saw three of the five Chase brothers sitting at the bar, including the lawyer. Benedict. My heart leapt.

Until the big one — Logan — charged over and hauled me away from Ruby and I squalled like a baby. He was fucking *scary*. Not the calm quiet kind of scary, like Evershaw, but enraged, rip-your-face-off scary. I fully expected to die, and then Val wouldn't have that to look forward to.

Except Benedict jumped up and bumped chests with his brother, shoving me behind him. I didn't mind in the least, since he had a lovely broad back to hide against, and he radiated warmth after the chill from the car. Lewis didn't believe in using the heat, apparently. So I leaned against Benedict and waited for the storm to blow over. And then I heard a semi-familiar voice, and leaned around the side of my large protector to say, "Charity lady?"

Her perfectly groomed eyebrows arched and I flushed, more than a little embarrassed. I should have remembered her name.

But she smiled and stepped forward to shake my hand, though she didn't get as far as she wanted because of the big dude's hold on her waist, and she had to both lean and stretch to touch me. I started to meet her in the middle but Benedict did the same thing, arms around me to keep me close. She rolled her eyes but pressed my fingers with hers. "It's Natalia, Eloise. It's lovely to see you. I was worried, when we didn't see you for a while."

I pushed away embarrassment. Lots of people needed a little help now and then. Going to a soup kitchen wasn't anything to be ashamed of. But I remembered being rough around the edges then, hating life a lot more and not able to control the scary mojo. "Sure, sorry I forgot your name."

I froze as the door burst open again and the two other Chase brothers came in, both with gold eyes and ready for trouble. Atticus straightened as he surveyed the situation and Edgar waved him off, then his gaze rested on me. Incredulity made him look younger than he really was. "Eloise?"

Well, damn. Benedict's arms tightened around me and that grumble started in his chest again. Atticus immediately ducked his head and held his hands up, backing up a step or two.

Natalia glanced between them, then back at me. She must have sensed my discomfort, I could see it in her eyes. But

Logan didn't care, glaring at the lawyer who still tried to hide me behind him. "End it, Benedict. We don't consort with criminals or the hyenas, got it? I don't want *that* in our family."

Benedict's shoulders broadened and Ruby started growling again. But it was Atticus who jumped forward, hands up. "Dude, don't. Don't piss her off."

Silence rocked through the bar and I tried to make myself very small even as panic roiled up in my stomach. Atticus knew at least a part of what I was, he knew why the fight organizers had me on retainer to referee. If they knew what I really was, they'd never help me. Ruby and Rafe would kick me out. No one liked gorgons.

Logan's nostrils flared. "I beg your pardon?"

"Logan, man, she's not — she's a —"

"Shut the fuck up," I said, jumping out and driving a finger into that massive chest. He was an undefeated street fighter but I could end him if I really wanted to. Which he knew very well, and tried to warn his brother. My hands shook and too much mojo curled through my brain and eyes. "Shut up about other people's secrets, Atticus."

He flushed but didn't look away from his brother, trying to sound calm. "Believe me, Logan. Let this one go. Don't piss her off."

Benedict caught my arm and drew me to his side once more. He took a deep breath, as if to assure himself I was still me, then he went stiff and held me at arm's length. "Why do you smell like Todd Evershaw?"

"For fuck's sake." I put a hand to my forehead and tried to collect my thoughts. "Could I just get a drink before we have to fucking talk about this?"

Ruby snapped, "Good idea," and pressed a shot glass into my hand. She downed three of her own before I managed to inhale mine. Then she pointed the knife-hand at me, some of her alpha fury spilling out and making the hair stand on the back of my neck. "Start talking, chickie."

I looked around at the collective audience, the silent pack members just waiting to be dismissed, and massaged my temples. "Somewhere else, if you don't mind?"

The BloodMoon alphas weren't pleased, and Ruby's patience hung on by a thread. She grabbed my shoulder and propelled me toward the stairs. "Get your shit upstairs and sit down. Benedict, Edgar — you may join her. Logan, it is probably best you go home," and she slanted a look at the charity lady.

The Chase alpha practically took Atticus by the ear and dragged his ass out the door like another misbehaving kid, with charity lady not far behind and the worried-looking Carter on her heels. Edgar raised his eyebrows at me and gestured at the back staircase. "Ladies first."

I didn't want to like him, but I did. I slanted a look at Ruby, though. "Seriously, do we —"

"Go," she growled, and I went.

The upstairs rooms were for pack business only, usually, with a large central living room and a few smaller bedrooms leading away from it. There were at least two bathrooms that I'd found; I desperately wanted another shower. And a nap. Just the thought of the bears made me shiver. Something draped over my shoulders and I jumped, grabbing the blanket that covered my shoulders. Benedict had a hearty scowl on his face as he nudged me toward one of the couches. "You're cold."

"I'm always cold," I said under my breath. It came from having ice in my heart, quicksilver in my veins. But I collapsed on the battered sofa, the brown leather smooth and soft as butter under my hands. I curled up against one arm and Benedict dropped next to me, still looking irritated.

Edgar took one of the armchairs, studying me with an indecipherable expression. Rafe and Ruby stormed up; though Rafe placed himself with deliberate care in another chair, Ruby paced and stomped around the edge of the room, her eyes throwing sparks almost as well as mine did. I double-checked my sunglasses. All the strong emotions flaring around made me nervous.

Rafe pressed his fingers together at his chin, cold calm settling around him. "What did Miles say?"

"Why don't we start at the beginning?" Edgar could also do the impassive, disinterested look remarkably well. I made a mental note to ask how he did that. I needed lessons in looking like I gave absolutely zero shits about anything.

Ruby growled, and the hair on her forehead started creeping toward her eyebrows. I held up my hands, sitting forward a little. "Jesus, okay. Fine. Everyone stay in their current form, okay? I can't handle any more of this posturing bullshit."

And four pairs of supernatural eyes landed on me. Since they were probably also at the end of their control, and a weirdo with silver eyes yelling at them probably didn't help. My head ached. I sighed, rubbing furiously at my temples. "Sorry. It's just — can I get some aspirin or something, Ruby?"

Edgar handed me the bottle of whisky, instead. I definitely liked him.

I took a deep breath and a deeper swig, easing back on the couch and ignoring that Benedict edged closer and spread another blanket across me. "I had a job to do for Val Thursday night, and I did it. I did it exactly like she said, but something went wrong and the money disappeared. She blames me for it. So I have — one more day," and my stomach dropped. Shit. "To either get her the money back or find her daughter. I dropped the money on SilverLine's territory, so Ruby and Rafe were kind enough to set up a meeting with Evershaw today."

"Fucking Miles Evershaw," Ruby said under her breath, teeth white and pointy as she whirled and made another circuit. She swiped at a shelf and knocked the contents to the floor.

I flinched, squinting behind the sunglasses, and the pain spiked to knives in my eyes. "When I got there, he said he wouldn't tell me what I asked unless I promised him a favor."

"Eloise," Rafe said, eyes darkening.

Flustered, I threw my hands up and drew my knees to my chest. "Well, fuck — if you know what happened, why am I repeating it?"

"Tell me," Edgar said, smooth as a silk garrote and just as dangerous. Calm brown eyes, mild and unthreatening, caught mine. Eased some of the tension from my head and eyes. "What did he do to you?"

Like he was some kind of pervy rapist. I shook my head, fatigue rolling over me until I wanted to just curl up on the sofa and sleep forever. Preferably with Benedict as a pillow or a blanket. Maybe both. "It wasn't that. He wanted to know — what I am, and when I wouldn't tell him, he got all alpha mad. Wouldn't let me look away and then I thought my head would explode, because of the — stuff in it. Todd jumped in and knocked me aside, but then he wouldn't stop smelling me. He said I smelled good."

A threatening grumble rose in Benedict and his arm snaked out to catch me, draw me close. I should have minded. I didn't, not really. He was a warm backrest I could lean against, and his fingers started working at the knots in my shoulders. My hair unraveled and spilled across his lap. "Sorry," I said, and tried to corral it back to someplace manageable. "Sometimes it has a mind of its own."

"Did your hair just —" Edgar started, a frown drawing wrinkles across his forehead.

I flushed, sinking lower. "I can't help it."

Ruby leaned her arms on the back of Rafe's chair, her attention on Benedict more than me. "I can't help this either," and she gestured at the spontaneous hair growth on her arms and forehead. "Keep talking."

I twined the hair around my fingers, dreaming of another hot shower. Maybe with Benedict. Much better than alone. I sighed, sadness creeping over me. "Miles said he wouldn't help me unless I promised him a favor. I didn't have any other choice. Val will kill me, or the jackals will kill me, or *you* might kill me," and I poked Benedict in the ribs.

"Me?" He rubbed the base of my head and I went boneless, almost sliding completely off the couch. Benedict sounded almost hurt. "How could you possibly think I would hurt you?"

"Because you're not afraid of me." The words slipped out before I could think to take them back, and then they hung there in the middle of the room.

His hands paused, then worked down toward my shoulders again. His tone was too deliberately casual for it to be an idle question, though I couldn't sense the trap. "What do you mean?"

Maybe if I mopped the floors again, Ruby would let me stay. She watched me with such a fierce frown, I kind of doubted it. "Everyone is afraid of me." It helped that I didn't really have to look at anyone as I leaned against Benedict; the other three were in my peripheral vision, but if I concentrated on the blanket across my lap, it was as if we were alone. "Everyone is. That's the only way I stay safe. If they're afraid of me, even a little bit, they won't hurt me."

"Why do they fear you?" This from Edgar, so smooth and patient. He was dangerous, probably more dangerous than anyone else in the room. He was the patient hunter, the one who would chase you for forty or eighty or a hundred miles until you died of exhaustion.

I shook my head and Benedict resumed working his fingers against the knot of tension at the base of my skull, around to behind my ears. He said quietly, "So you agreed to the favor?"

"I had to," I repeated, trying to convince myself as much as him. "So he told me the bears had been on their territory, right near where the money disappeared, and he said they might know what was going on."

"The bears." This from Rafe in his flat, creepy voice, and I shivered. He pinched the bridge of his nose. "Did he say which ones?"

Benedict draped another blanket over me, frowning as I fumbled and pulled the piece of paper from where I'd stuck it in my pocket. I felt cocooned and sleepy, him a furnace at my back and side with layers of blankets all around me. I cleared my throat. "The polar bear and the brown bear. Do you know them?"

Ruby started pacing again, throwing her hands in the air and muttering under her breath. Rafe took a deep breath and shook his head. "If they took whoever you're looking for, Eloise, chances are there won't be much left. The bears aren't very nice people."

My throat closed up. I'd assumed the same, but to hear the normally optimistic Rafe say that Lacey was probably dead made it too real. I had to move the sunglasses so I could wipe some moisture from my eyes, clearing my throat. "That's what I — that's what I figured. I just need to know for sure."

Benedict drew me closer, fingers working through my hair and kneading my scalp, but he spoke to his brother. "Ed, I thought Kaiser and his guys were doing security these days."

"They are. Bodyguard work mostly, from what I hear, but a variety of other services as well. What are you thinking?"

Benedict took a deep breath and I nearly sat up as his chest expanded. He leaned down and inhaled from my hair as well. "Kidnapping and ransom isn't their style. And they might not care about territory, as long as they can roam where they want, but they'd damn well know violating Evershaw's territory on behalf of the hyenas and whoever paid them to take the girl would jeopardize everything else they have going on. It's too stupid for them."

I tried to sit up. "It wasn't the bears?"

"They might have been providing security," Edgar said, then glanced at his phone with a frown. "Bodyguard services for whoever showed up for the cash. They don't like getting involved in other people's drama, but they're also pretty serious about keeping agreements."

"Would they help?" Hope gave me enough energy to push back the blankets and try to rise, but Benedict's arm looped around my waist.

Ruby scowled. "What, so you can owe them a favor, too? Damn it, girl, Todd Evershaw is *still* calling me, trying to figure out if you're spoken for."

"She is," Edgar said, real casual.

I blinked as she slapped the back of his head, and fully expected the lion to jump up and roar about the disrespectful wolf. Except Edgar only smiled and kept fussing with his phone. Ruby pointed at me, or maybe Benedict. "Look, chickie. I like you a lot but I'm not going to war with SilverLine for you. I can't. So you've got to figure out how you want to play it. Todd Evershaw, despite being Miles' brother, is a good guy. Benedict is a lawyer, so make of that what you will. And if you want to stay a free agent, fine, but give me a head's up so I don't end up with a bar full of men, moping around and crying in their beer."

I had to take my sunglasses off to squint at her. "Wait, *what*?"

It was Ruby's turn to rub her temples. "Babe, Benedict likes you. Todd, apparently, likes you. Is there one you prefer?"

My heart sank and heat flushed my cheeks. Words wouldn't form.

Rafe started to smile and ducked his head, and Edgar looked on the verge of laughing out loud. I tried to sit up and collect my dignity. "That can wait, and it doesn't involve any of you. Can you please tell me how to get to the bears' house?"

"Why yes, Goldilocks," Edgar said, and the laugh escaped. Even Ruby couldn't keep a straight face. The Chase security chief fixed me with a stern look, though. "They are not the kind of guys that you just walk up to and start demanding things from, Eloise."

I collapsed forward and covered my face with my hands. "Jesus Christ. I just need to find Lacey. By tomorrow. Before Val kills me."

"She won't kill you," Benedict said, gathering me once again to his side and straightening the blankets to cover me up completely. "I'll go with you to meet with Kaiser. He's the alpha for the bears. He might be able to help you."

"But what if he can't?" I looked at him, then his brother, then Ruby and Rafe. Fear surged in my throat before I remembered not to meet their eyes. "What if he won't help me and I can't find Lacey and she's dead? What then? I can't pay Val her ten grand back and I can't pay back another loan to Bridger, she — her price is too high, I can't do it. How am I —"

Benedict hushed me, smoothing my hair out of the way so he could massage up the back of my neck. "Deep breaths. We'll fix it. We'll find your friend, and if we don't, the money is easy."

"Easy for you to say," I shot back, bitterness making me unkind even as his magic hands melted the ache out of my brain. "You've *got* money, you don't have to go to some damn loan shark if —"

"Yes," Benedict said, slow and patient. "I do have a lot of money. I will give you some of that money, and then you can pay Szdoka back."

"But —" I cut off, cheeks burning as I straightened and faced him, and noticed that Rafe and Ruby had disappeared. "But why would —"

"Because I like you," he said, and leaned forward to kiss the tip of my nose. "And you're worried about a lot of stuff. So we pay Szdoka back so you can have more time to find your friend. Okay? We'll go talk to the bears tomorrow. Kaiser owes me a favor."

I frowned, trying to concentrate as I looked at him and then Edgar. Edgar shoved to his feet. "I'm calling it a night, and I'm taking the car. So you're both stuck here. Ben, I'll have Carter drop a car off for you tomorrow morning."

Benedict didn't seem to mind, playing with my hair. "One of the SUVs. Just in case. And some cash."

I looked between them, trying to keep up when it felt like half the conversation remained unspoken. Edgar looked at me, a hint of a smile softening his expression. "How much money does Val expect you to turn over?"

"Ten thousand," I whispered.

"Interest?"

"Not that I know of?"

Edgar straightened, smacked Benedict's shoulder, and clattered down the stairs, whistling. I stared after them, then looked at Benedict. "What the hell is going on?"

He yawned and stretched, arm across my shoulders. "First, let's talk about why you took all my clothes when you left this morning."

I sank a little lower and let one of the blankets creep over my nose. Right.

chapter 12

Her cheeks flushed immediately and Benedict worked to keep a straight face. She even brought one of the blankets up to hide her face until only those wide silver eyes were visible. Mesmerizing. Her voice reached him, small and muffled. "Well, I didn't want you running after me. Just in case Val had her people waiting outside to grab me."

Half a smile escaped before Benedict could reinforce his stern expression, and he had to look away before he laughed. "You stole my clothes and left me naked in a hotel room to protect me from the hyenas?"

"Yes." Even in one word, he heard a bit of a giggle.

Benedict rubbed his forehead, then leaned forward until he could have rested his chin on her knee. "While I appreciate the sentiment, don't do it again." Then he tweaked the end of her nose through the blanket and smiled. "Edgar will be screwing with me for years over that."

Those silver eyes half-closed and she yawned, sinking lower on the leather couch. He just wanted to sit there and watch her. Maybe feed her. Touch that crazy hair that seemed to reach out for him. Instead, he pushed to his feet and held out a hand to help her up. "Kaiser and his guys get up early, so we'd better meet them early. You ready for bed?"

She hesitated, but eventually stood, looking a little rumpled. Benedict folded the blankets and put them across the back of the couch and headed for one of the bedrooms, expecting her to stake a claim on the bathroom and another room. Instead, she followed him into his room and started taking off her clothes.

He blinked. "Eloise, what are you doing?"

She froze, shirt half-over her head. "What do you mean?"

"I mean," he said, moving forward to help replace the shirt so he could see her face. She looked resigned more than anything. Resigned and tired. "Do you want to sleep here with me, or in the other room?"

"But —" Another yawn almost cracked her jaw, and the long dark tendrils of her hair floated up from her shoulders. "If you're loaning me the money, how am I supposed to pay you back?"

His heart sank. She couldn't think the loan came with strings attached, and certainly not an expectation that she would put out. Benedict fought to keep from stepping back or recoiling or showing any of his revulsion at the idea of trading his money for sex. "Baby," he said, reaching out to catch her shoulders. "If you need the money, it's a gift."

"No." She shook her head, backing up out of reach and bumping into the battered dresser against the wall. "No, I don't take charity."

Chasing Trouble

"It's not charity," he said. "A gift. And if you want to pay it back, then we can figure something out, but I can tell you right now, it won't include you sleeping with me out of obligation."

Her face flushed and she chewed her bottom lip, not meeting his eyes.

As the silence stretched, his heart sank. "At the hotel. You only fucked me to pay me back for lunch?"

Eloise flinched, turning away, and he felt lower than the lowest snake. That amazing night was purchased with a fifty dollar lunch. Benedict pressed the heels of his hands to his eyes and turned away, walking into the living room before he said or did something he couldn't take back. A growl started in his chest despite that he tried to swallow it down. The lion was not pleased, wanted to take her in the bedroom and show her why she couldn't put a price on what they shared. But he felt absolutely low.

"It wasn't that," she said, and followed him back into the living room. Benedict held up a hand to keep her from getting too close, and she stopped short. Eloise cleared her throat. "I thought you were like the others. I'm sorry."

"So it was that," he said. Benedict felt flat, as if she'd gutted him. "It was ... transactional?"

"Don't look at me like that," she whispered, hands up near her face.

Benedict faced her, for the first time questioning if everyone else were correct and Eloise only wanted his money. "Like what?"

"Like I betrayed you." Those silver eyes devoured him, the hair rose in a cloud, and a hint of red rimmed her eyes. "Please. I'm sorry. I thought that's what it was, but then you touched me and —"

She cut off abruptly as the wobble in her chin grew too strong and her voice shook along with it. Benedict gave up and sat on the couch, head in his hands. He'd never paid for sex. Ever. He'd never taken advantage of a woman who needed help, would never dream of pursuing a relationship with such dynamics. And the fact that she thought that about him, even for a moment, shook everything he believed about himself. Made him question every relationship he'd ever had.

He took a deep breath, still rubbing his forehead. "Eloise, I might need a minute."

She looked as crushed as he felt, and retreated. Sat in one of the arm chairs and stared at him as if she could will him into doing something. He tensed. Maybe she could. He still didn't know exactly what she was, maybe she'd manipulated him. Benedict didn't look at her. "How else did you convince me? Did you use some weird magic on me? Get me to do what you want?"

Her lips parted but she started shaking her head, more and more vehemently in his peripheral vision. "No. I thought you would run away. When I'm angry, people just run. But you stayed. You stayed right there, and I couldn't —" She pulled at her hair, angrily wrapped it up in a bun when it tangled around her fingers, and she shoved to her feet again. Paced around the coffee table, close enough to bump his knees. "I don't think I did. I didn't mean to."

When he sat back, shaking his head, she lurched forward and almost tripped over the table. "I didn't mean to, I swear. If I did, it was because you — you..." She chewed her lip desperately, hands out. "I'm cold. I'm always cold. Except when you were there. It's because what I am — there's ice inside me. There's so much coldness and I can crush it down, hold it down for a while but then other people get mean or angry and it just sort of — comes out. And then I have ice in my eyes and my brain and my veins and it has to go somewhere."

He watched the silver swirling in her eyes, as it pooled and then dripped onto her cheek. His heart sank, the lion demanded he comfort her, but he couldn't move. The man couldn't do it yet. Eloise cleared her throat, her voice remarkably steady despite that another tear snuck out. "Every other time, someone gets hurt. Me or someone else, the ice has to go somewhere. Except — except that night, when I was with you, it didn't. You warmed it out of me." And her entire face went red.

Benedict refused to admit it was an ego boost to think he'd heated her right through. Not that any of it made any sense. He rubbed his forehead, trying to remain aloof despite the unhappiness radiating from her. "I need you to be one hundred percent honest with me, right now. We need to have a conversation about this stuff and I need to trust that you mean every word. Otherwise I'm not sure how this —" and he waved a hand between them, not wanting to put into words what he thought they'd shared. "—would work. Okay?"

She shifted her feet, uneasy, but finally nodded, retreating to stand behind one of the chairs as if it offered some protection from his questions.

Benedict rubbed his jaw, watching her. "What are you?"

Eloise wiped her cheeks and plucked at the seams on the chair cushion. "I'm a gorgon. Part gorgon."

"Gorgon?" He just looked at her, waiting for more.

She made a flustered noise, the color creeping up her cheeks. "Gran was a medusa. My mom was part, and she thought if she bred with a man who was something else, I wouldn't get any of the nastiness from Gran. It didn't work."

Bred. The word disturbed him. It was far too clinical for an intimate process, a miracle that produced Eloise. But he kept his lawyer face on, remained impassive. This could all be another act. "So what was your father?"

"I don't know, exactly. Not human. Not shifter, that I know of." She shrugged, not quite meeting his eyes. "He wasn't around. Might have just been a donor."

Benedict cringed inside, to think of any man abandoning his family like that. Especially a daughter, lost and uncertain. "So that's why you ended up in foster care?"

"How did you —"Those silver eyes flashed and some of the misery faded into irritation. "How did you know?"

"Natalia knew a friend of yours at the soup kitchen. She spilled the beans about you and foster care. The group home."

Eloise shook her head, rubbed her upper arms and moved around the room, more of a wander and less of a pace. "I was in rough shape back then. More so than now," and she gave him a half-smile before wheeling about and facing away. "I couldn't really control the mojo, so every foster home that took me sent me back after a couple of weeks. They thought I was creepy or dangerous. So I ended up in a group home full of predators." Her hair uncurled from the bun and created a curtain across her face, hiding her expression. "It went about as well as you would expect."

Benedict could imagine. He'd done an internship during law school with family law, and occasionally provided pro bono services for child advocates. He'd seen the results of the foster care system first hand. So her view of relationships as inherently transactional wasn't really a surprise. He took a deep breath.

But she wasn't finished. Eloise clenched her hands into fists. "But I survived it. I survived. I'm never going back to that place. I'm in control of my emotions, I'm in control of this — *thing* that I am. It does not define who I am. I'm not just a monster."

The lion grumbled his support, and Benedict struggled to find the appropriate words. At length, he managed, "You could never be a monster, Eloise."

"I am. At least part." She flapped a hand to dismiss whatever argument he might have offered. "I'm a monster. That's okay. It took a long time to admit that. I just have to control it. Stuff it down."

"What if you didn't stuff it down?" He sat forward, elbows on knees, and considered one of the year-old magazines on the coffee table. "For us, not shifting just makes the shift less controllable. The longer we go without taking the other form, the harder it is to remember being human. Maybe it's the same for you."

"When you shift, you don't automatically kill someone, do you?" She glanced at him and away, fighting to contain her hair once more. "If I go full gorgon, people die. Immediately. It's not a pretty thing. It hurts. To see someone turn to stone. Exactly as they were the moment I looked at them."

A shiver ran through her and he almost missed the desperate wipe at her cheeks again. Benedict eased to his feet. "Is that why you were surprised I'm not afraid of you?"

"Everyone's afraid of me," she said, low and cold. "It's just a matter of time. Even Ruby — she pretends like she's not afraid, but she is. And Atticus, who's the best streetfighter in the entire league — he flinches if I look in his direction."

Benedict cracked one knuckle at a time. "You know Atticus from the fights?"

A brief glance at him, then a bitter laugh. "Well, since we're being honest, yeah. I'm on retainer for one of the leagues, in case someone goes full berserk. I can paralyze them or kill them, depending on how bad it is. They pay pretty well, usually, but lately it seems like Val has a tax on it."

He wanted to punch Val Szdoka in the face the next time he saw her. Benedict looked at his watch. Almost eleven.

Eloise didn't notice, didn't seem to care, staring blindly at a painting on the far wall. "And you too. You might not be afraid of me, but you don't like what I am. It's okay. I'll pay you back somehow."

"Eloise," he said, sounding more tired than he felt. "I don't like what you did. It's different."

"Right." She cleared her throat, turning on her heel and heading to the back bedroom. The one farthest away from where he'd been going to sleep. "I'm going to turn in. I'll be up to help Ruby mop the floors. I can find the bears on my own."

The door shut before he could get a single word out, and Benedict stared at it with no idea what to do. It made sense. It all made sense, every last word of it. That didn't make it any easier to rid himself of the uneasiness of their first encounter. He didn't know if they could recover from that. If she would give him the chance to recover.

chapter 13

I woke with a massive headache beating behind my eyes, the result of crying instead of the mojo, for once. Lesson learned. Never admit to sleeping with a guy to pay him back for something nice. Maybe normal people didn't think that way. Maybe that was something else to thank Gran for. I took a longer shower than normal, just to avoid going into the living room and potentially facing the humiliation of talking to Benedict. Clearly he wanted nothing else to do with me — whether that was because of the sex or me being a monster didn't really matter.

I braided my hair back tightly and used a few loose bobby pins to secure more of it. I couldn't face the bears with random tendrils sneaking out. It seemed to be getting wilder with each passing day. I'd never had this much trouble with the hair before. My hands paused as I added another hairband to the braid. Just since I met Benedict.

Maybe he wasn't good for my control. Maybe he kept the ice back but made everything else worse. I scrubbed my face with cold water, furious with myself. Stupid mistake. Stupid ridiculous fairytale mistake. Monsters didn't get happy endings. Monsters died, the hero saved the real princess, and everyone lived happily ever after.

Tears burned my sinuses again, a terrible fiery pain compared to the icy one, and I washed my face again. Put on the mask that saved my ass in foster care, and marched out of that room like I didn't care about anything.

Ruby waited for me downstairs, along with her brother and Benedict. Their heated discussion silenced as I walked into the main area, and all three looked at me. I knew they'd been talking about me, arguing about me. Probably about who got to turn me over to Val. So I slung my bag over my shoulder and nodded to the three of them. Time to be an adult. Hike up my big girl panties and deal with the consequences of my actions. "Thanks for letting me stay, Ruby. I'm gonna go find Val before she finds me."

"What the fuck are you talking about?" Rafe moved around the bar, eyes narrowed. "Why are you leaving?"

"Look, you guys don't need me around." I smiled at much as I dared. "The hyenas are going to start some shit over this, and I don't want it to blow back on you. It's fine. So instead of you guys having to come up with a reason to kick me out, I'll just go. Really, I —"

"What the hell did you do?" This time it was Ruby, but she glared at Benedict.

He shook his head, watching me. "Why are you really leaving, Eloise?"

"Like I said." My words cracked and I had to swallow a knot of regret. "I'm bad luck, this won't work out. I'd rather leave now than get booted later."

Ruby punched his shoulder. "You fucking ass, what did you —"

"It's not his fault." I had to pitch my voice over the growl emanating from Benedict, but I held up my hands to cut them both off. "It's my fault. I did something stupid. He's right to be mad. It's fine, Ruby. If you knew the truth, you wouldn't want me around either."

"Bullshit." Rafe strode after me and caught my arm, jerking me back. "I don't care what you think you did, you're not going on your own to face Val Szdoka or the bears. It's not right."

Before I could open my mouth to argue, Rafe disappeared. Staggered back the entire length of the bar, and instead Benedict stood next to me, scowling at where the wolf braced against the wall. "Don't put your hands on her."

Then he faced me and an old part of my brain told me to get very still so the predator wouldn't notice me. It was too late, though. His eyes were liquid gold as he caught my shoulders. "Damn it, Eloise. I'm not mad. I was confused, maybe a little hurt, but I'm not mad. Just don't do it again."

I stared at his chest, not entirely sure I believed him. I wanted to believe him so badly my chest ached, but my luck was never that good. My voice came out too small. "You said it wouldn't work."

The grumbly noise in his chest rolled through me and he drew me suddenly close to him, pressing his nose to my hair. "I don't know if it will work. I hope it will. We're learning, aren't we? I mean, you left my clothes this time. Stayed all the way to the morning. That's progress, right?"

Layla Nash

I wanted to smile but my cheeks wouldn't work.

"You aren't a monster," he said, so soft I hoped Rafe wouldn't hear. Then Benedict kissed my forehead, spun me around, and marched me to sit at the bar in front of a plate of eggs and pancakes. "Now eat. We meet Kaiser in thirty minutes."

Ruby eyed the lion, then tapped the bar near my plate as I shoveled eggs into my mouth. "Okay, chickie. Be careful with the bears. Even with superman over there to help you out. Kaiser is a good dude, but some of his guys are a little ... unstable. Keep your sunglasses and your game face on. Got it?"

"Game face," I repeated around a mouthful of pancakes, nodding. "Right. What kind of bear is he?"

Rafe rubbed his shoulder as he stalked around the bar, shooting Benedict an irritated look. "He's a grolar bear. And he's still less of a dick than your boyfriend."

"Don't put your hands on a woman," Benedict said, sounding unruffled.

And I blushed, because he didn't correct the 'boyfriend' part. I cleared my throat. "What the hell is a grolar bear?"

"His ma was a polar bear," Ruby said. She poured coffee into a brandy tumbler and slid it in front of me. "And his da was a grizzly bear. So he's a grolar. Not a teddy bear, not a care bear — he's a real fucking bear."

I made a face as I sipped the coffee, almost burning my palms through the glass. "Will he help me?"

Ruby and Rafe traded looks, then she eyed me critically. "Probably. He's got a soft spot for troublemakers. Which is why he's got a handful of misfit bears around him."

"Great," I said under my breath. I finished inhaling the breakfast and paused for a moment, debating whether a burp would turn into something more substantial. Luckily everything stayed where it was supposed to, and I followed Benedict out the front to a waiting SUV.

He handed me some sunglasses, "Try these," and opened the car door for me.

I examined the glasses as he started driving, putting them on to appreciate the coverage and checking in the mirror to make sure they hid my eyes completely. Before I could thank him, Benedict fussed with the radio. "We've only known each other a few days, Eloise, but I would like to know you better."

"Oh." I cleared my throat and willed away a hysterical giggle that welled up in my chest.

Before I could compose myself, he slid a sideways glance at me. "Normally that's where you say you'd like to know me better, too."

"I, uh, would like to know you better. Too."

"Well, now I can't tell if you mean it." He sighed. "Shouldn't have given you those sunglasses."

I couldn't contain a smile, relaxing in the seat. "Nope. Rookie mistake."

He smiled at the windshield, and the rest of the ride, neither of us said anything.

He parked the car in a rundown part of town not too far from where Miles Evershaw headquartered his business. Benedict didn't get out right away but instead picked up my hand. He studied my fingers, examining my nails and palm and knuckles. His voice registered as a slight puff of air against my skin. "I don't know how it is with your people, Eloise, but mine usually know right away when they find someone they like. I don't want to scare you off by getting too serious. Just give me a sign when you're ready, okay?"

Layla Nash

I watched him watching my hand. My fingers curled over his. "Okay."

"Okay," he repeated, then pressed his lips to the soft skin on the inside of my wrist. A chill ran through me at the warm brush of his mouth, the tenderness in his touch. Then he winked at me and got out of the car.

I hopped out before he made it around the car. "But I open my own door, got it?"

Benedict sketched an elaborate bow and offered his arm in a courtly gesture. "Shall we enter the bear's den?"

"Let's," I said with a laugh, though I didn't take his arm. Benedict shoved his hands in his pockets and ambled along beside me. As the late fall wind cut through me, I reconsidered snuggling up next to him, but it was a short walk to the crumbling building.

chapter 14

The bears definitely shared a realtor with Miles Evershaw. The ramshackle industrial building hid a large, open interior behind a crumbling facade, which the bears filled with weight machines, a makeshift boxing ring, and some couches that looked as though real bears used them for napping.

Benedict rang the bell next to the glass-front door and a buzzer rang to unlock the door. A young man, maybe in his mid-twenties, approached to greet us, blinking and rubbing his eyes under a shock of black hair. He smiled through a yawn. "Benedict? I'm Owen. The boss is out back," and he jerked his chin toward the rear of the building and a massive metal door.

Benedict shook his hand before following him through the building, but the lawyer didn't say anything. Irritation colored my tone more than I wanted. "I'm Eloise, by the way. Nice to meet you."

Owen lumbered along, still blinking. He inclined his head but didn't try to take my hand. "Nice to meet you, Eloise.

Usually we don't address another man's mate until introduced, so..." and he gave Benedict a drowsy but reproachful look.

"I'm not —" I started just as Benedict put me in a gentle headlock and said over me, "My mistake, Owen. I forgot about the ursine code."

"Not a problem," Owen said mildly, pushing open the enormous steel door to reveal a backyard almost as large as the whole first floor of the building. Maybe we'd woken Owen from his winter hibernation, because nothing else explained the lackadaisical attitude.

Almost a third of the backyard hosted an above-ground infinity pool, cycling water through with a distinctive splashing, but a patch of dirt and pile of scarred logs dominated the rest of the space. Most of the logs sported deep gouges and splintering. As I considered the size of the animal capable of raking three inch deep furrows in solid wood, Owen tapped on the side of the pool with about as much energy as molasses in February.

A dark head popped up out of the water and I yelped, stumbling back and almost falling on my ass. A bear. A real goddamn bear. Owen blinked as he looked around for the threat just as Benedict grabbed me up off the ground and shoved me behind him. The giant bear, easily ten feet tall, rose to its back legs and sprayed water as it shook out its golden blonde fur. Owen ducked and even Benedict turned his face to avoid the deluge.

I peeked around Benedict just in time to see the bear curl in on itself, then disappear into the water and stand up as a man. My heart tried to break through my ribs. Holy shit. The massive bear turned into an equally massive man, larger than

Atticus and certainly taller and broader than Benedict, who was built for speed more than brawn.

The bear winced and climbed out of the pool as he toweled off. "Thought I'd get in an early swim. What can I do for you, Benedict?"

The man was bare-ass naked but didn't seem to care as he shook Benedict's hand. My cheeks burned as I tried to concentrate on the man's face when confronted with the washboard abs and impressive package. Benedict kept me close to his side. "Kaiser, thanks for meeting. This is my friend Eloise."

The bear, Kaiser, smiled and I automatically smiled back. Maybe Rafe was wrong and this Kaiser guy was a teddy bear. He lumbered over and pressed my fingers delicately, dark eyes kind. "Ms. Eloise, nice to meet you."

My cheeks heated more and I stumbled over a few words meant to thank him for seeing us, particularly with his nude Adonis form and an impressive amount of chest hair right in front of me. God help me if I sneezed, we might end up on third base by accident. Benedict grumbled in his throat and slid his arm around my waist.

Kaiser chuckled and nodded at the metal door. "We can talk in my office." He led the way — well, his perfect butt led the way and I bit my lip. Luckily Owen handed him another towel that Kaiser wrapped around his waist, then the sleepy bear shut the door behind us and disappeared into another part of the building.

Benedict tugged on the end of my braid as he muttered, "Enjoying the view?"

"You don't saunter around naked as a jaybird," I said, then gave Kaiser a bright smile as he held open the door to an office behind the boxing ring. "Thank you."

Layla Nash

The bear waited until we sat in front of his desk before taking his place behind the desk, still wearing only a towel. "So what brings you to my den?"

Uneasiness bubbled in my stomach once more, despite the apparent friendliness of this particular bear. What if he didn't tell me what happened Thursday night? He was my last chance to figure this out before Val came for my head. I took a deep breath and braced my hands on my knees, not quite daring to meet his gaze as I spoke. "Thursday night, I dropped a bag of money near Aaron's Chili Bowl for Val Szdoka. Someone took her daughter and demanded a ransom. I didn't see who picked up the money because a bunch of cops came through, but when I went back, the money was gone and Val didn't have her daughter. I'm trying to find my friend and figure out who's got her. The SilverLine pack said they chased bears away from that part of their territory on Thursday night, so we were hoping — I was hoping you might be able to tell me more about who took the money and what happened afterward."

Kaiser snorted a laugh. "Miles Evershaw said he chased off bears? Right." He shook his head and frowned at a chalkboard on the wall next to his desk. Apparently he could decipher the hieroglyphics written on it, because he frowned more. "That would have been Axel and Malcolm. Mal is out on another job, but Axel's around."

He picked up the phone on his desk but hesitated, eying me critically. "You got steady nerves, girl?"

"I work for the hyenas," I said. "I'll be fine."

"Okay. Just — stay calm." He looked at Benedict with less concern, "You too, lion," then said into the phone, "Get in my office."

Then he hung up and rubbed his jaw, his head tilted as he studied me. "I know you from somewhere. I don't recognize you but you smell familiar."

Benedict grumbled, and tension gathered in his shoulders as he took up all of the chair he occupied as well as half of my breathing room. I felt small and rather delicate sitting in the tiny room with a bear and a lion.

"The fights, probably," I said with a sigh. Of course all of the people mixed up in Val Szdoka's dirty business were also involved at least part-time in the illegal street-fighting.

A smile tugged at the bear's lips. "That can't be it."

"It is." I took off the sunglasses so he could see my eyes; most of them only remembered my eyes. "Bridger pays me to be security sometimes."

"Security." Then he leaned across the desk to peer at my eyes. Cold gathered in my eyes at the challenge, and Kaiser sat back. A huffing noise rolled out of his chest and through the air, bouncing off me. Then he nodded once and gestured at the boxing ring behind me. "If you ever want to practice stopping charging bear..." He raised his eyebrows.

I almost laughed. "Thanks for the offer, but I'm trying to minimize —"

The rest of my words disappeared in a squeak as I glanced back at the ring and faced instead an angry, half-naked Viking.

He filled the doorway next to Benedict, radiating aggression by posture and breathing alone. His blue eyes swept the room, measuring each of us. I scooted my chair back, glad Benedict was both a speedbump between us and looking ready to brawl if the Viking got a step closer. The giant blonde growled deep in his chest as he squinted at me with icy blue eyes.

Kaiser sniffed and rubbed his nose. "Axel, they got some questions about the job you did on Thursday."

Axel inhaled deeply, nostrils flared, then folded his arms over his chest. "Okay."

Benedict didn't relinquish his chair or give any hint he was tense, bouncing his foot as if it were any normal business meeting. But the muscles corded across the back of his neck and shoulders, and he kept himself broadly between me and the threat. "We'd like to know who hired you, and what they hired you to do."

"Can't. Bad for business." A hint of white teeth showed as he inhaled again, mouth open to taste the air. His gaze landed on me like a ton of bricks. "Who are you?"

So apparently the bear code for asking about someone else's mate didn't apply to polar bears. Benedict started growling loudly enough that the hairs on my arms stood up. I refused to be discomfited. Ice condensed around my eyes and the scary mojo drifted up at the hint of a threat. "I'm Eloise."

"Just Eloise?"

"Just Eloise." I folded my arms over my chest. "I left a bag of money behind Aaron's Chili Bowl to pay a ransom for my friend, Val Szdoka's daughter Lacey. Someone picked it up but Lacey is still missing, probably hurt. I want to find Lacey but the trail ends with you."

"Brave for such a small thing," he said, so deep in his chest I felt it in my bones. His head tilted and a violet sheen covered his eyes. "Walk into a bear's den and make demands? Ballsy."

Benedict lurched up but I grabbed his shoulder and yanked him back to the chair. My shoulders objected but I didn't want him getting caught in the mojo shrapnel. And part of me wondered why Kaiser didn't get the polar bear to shut up and obey. My chin dropped as the mojo swirled up and coalesced behind my eyes. The braid hanging down my back lifted, individual tendrils working free to stand up around me in a heady cloud. My voice dropped an octave but I fought to remain aloof and unconcerned. "Kaiser, do you fancy a bear-shaped statue for your waiting room? Perhaps he can guard your front door."

Axel's eyes narrowed. "You're not —"

"If you want to take your chances, Axel, go ahead." Kaiser fiddled with a rusty drawer in his desk. "But she does security for Bridger. If she doesn't kill you, the lion will," and he nodded at where Benedict sprouted hair from elbows to fingers.

I didn't take my eyes off the Viking. The debate played out across his face, then his eyes faded once more to pale blue. He didn't look happy about it, upper lip lifting in a snarl. "The hyenas paid us."

"No, they paid the ransom to get Lacey back. The jackals might have —"

"It was hyenas." The muscles in his forearm jumped. "We escorted four hyenas to the location. They met someone there, dragged him away, then one of them picked up a bag. That was it. Hyenas. Didn't see anyone else."

The world slowed down. A clock ticking on the wall echoed in my ears. Pressure built behind my eyes as the cold didn't dissipate, but grew stronger. "Which hyenas?"

Axel shook his head. "Didn't ask."

"Female?"

"All of them."

I nodded, staring past him. A set-up. Val set me up. Lacey, too. A rushing sound filled my ears. And Val wanted to hold me responsible for the money and for Lacey's disappearance.

As I stared at Axel's chest, Benedict cleared his throat. "Would you recognize the hyenas if you saw them again?"

The polar bear's lip wrinkled again but he answered grudgingly. "Probably. Scent would be better."

As I remained frozen, Benedict nudged me. "Do you have a picture of Val's people? On your phone?"

Still worried mostly about not letting the scary mojo explode my eyes, I unlocked my phone and handed it to the lawyer. Benedict flipped across the screen, then handed it to Axel. "Anyone here jog your memory?"

The weight of their collective attention was too much. I lurched to my feet, "Excuse me a moment," and shoved past Benedict's restraining hands and Axel's bulk to escape the office. Stars spotted my vision and I struggled with the door to the backyard.

Thank Medusa no one followed me, though I lacked the strength to shut the door behind me. I clutched my head and dropped to sit on my heels in the chilly morning air. My face numbed from my eyebrows down until my skin cracked and my teeth ached. Set up. Goddamn Val. Trapping me with some bullshit about Lacey eloping and needing my help. I should have known. I should have seen it.

It was a stupid mistake to trust Lacey, knowing she was Val's daughter. Val set me up from the beginning, put all the chess pieces in place so she could eventually tighten the noose. Maybe Lacey really left on her own and Val used it as a convenient excuse to hold me accountable for the money. My braid fell apart completely and long locks of hair floated around me, twined thick as snakes. I pressed the heels of my hands against my eyes. Had to keep it together. Had to save the rage for Val herself.

Chasing Trouble

Val would learn not to threaten a gorgon. I hated the monster side of me, but the gorgon excelled at getting even. Protecting us. I chewed my lip and shoved to my feet, pacing the perimeter of the yard. A plan. I needed a plan before I faced Val. I needed more information. If the four hyenas hired the bears to protect them, they expected trouble.

Trouble from me, maybe. I groaned and gripped my sides as the cold traveled down my throat and spread into my lungs.

Or — trouble from the jackals. I stopped short. Cal. Cal ended up in the hospital, or so he claimed. Maybe that was part of the ruse as well. And if the hyenas beat him — if he was the one they met and dragged away — then he would know something. His pack might know something. Val long complained of the jackals and their threat to her territory and interests.

She killed two birds with one stone, it seemed.

I howled, hands clenched at my sides, and the cold burst out of my eyes and slammed into the logs balanced on the far side of the yard. Pain blinded me and I went to my knees. The monster took control and everything else faded.

chapter 15

Both the bears watched Eloise flee the office without expression, then Axel frowned down at the phone as he swiped. Benedict watched where she'd gone, straining to hear anything, and his muscles vibrated with the effort of remaining in his chair. His lion only wanted to chase her, to comfort her, to dispose of whatever pained her.

But she needed to know who among the hyenas betrayed her. So he sat in the office even as a yowl bounced off the metal door from outside and his lion snarled in sympathy. Kaiser frowned as he sat forward. "Is she okay?"

"Yes." Benedict didn't take his eyes off the phone. He concentrated on remaining calm. "If her control slips, it's best if she's outside. Alone."

He only guessed that were the case.

Axel grunted, then offered the phone back to Benedict. "These two definitely. Didn't see the others."

Benedict sent the photo to his phone, so he'd remember it, then paused as he started to stand. Eloise reappeared in the doorway and Axel eased back a step, closer to Kaiser. Eloise wore the sunglasses and concealed most of her face with a scarf, but nothing could hide the floating cloud of hair around her head.

The grolar bear blinked. "Your, uh —"

"I know." Her voice carried an edge. "I might have damaged some of your logs. Out back. I apologize."

Kaiser raised his hands. "Damage as many as you want, darlin'. We have a new shipment coming in next week."

A smile tugged at the corner of her mouth, but disappeared when Benedict held out her phone. "Do you recognize them, Eloise?"

A strange high-pitched, eerie noise welled up in her chest and hurt his ears. Her fingers tightened around it until the plastic cracked, but she didn't seem to notice. She stared at it until her lips curled back in a snarl.

"I take it you know them," Axel said, sharing a look with his fellow bear.

Benedict held his breath as he pried the phone out of her hand. Her skin took on a greenish-bluish tinge, and her hair tangled itself into serpent-sized groups. Just like a damn medusa statue. "Babe. Take a breath."

Nothing. He touched her arm, let his palm rest against her until the ice under her skin thawed. She blinked, then looked back at him. "The one on the left is Lorraine, Val's daughter. The other one is Heba, Val's niece."

Then silence. Benedict didn't release her arm as he faced Kaiser and nodded. "Thank you for your assistance. We'll let you know how things ... turn out."

He wanted to get her out of there before Eloise cracked completely. Regardless of whether she hurt him or the bears or just herself, he needed to keep her moving. He didn't know what happened to gorgons when they were enraged to the point of madness, but it looked as though Eloise were one cross word away from being stone herself. Benedict nudged her toward the door, also nodding to the grim polar bear as Axel followed them out of the office.

Axel studied Eloise as she stalked to the front door, every movement jerky and stiff. Benedict put her phone away and paused at the door, another thought occurring to him as he surveyed the weight machines and boxing ring. "Would you allow others to work out here? A lion, perhaps?"

The giant bear smirked, "Sure, little buddy. We'll take it easy on you."

Benedict straightened his shoulders and scowled at the dick. "I'm a precision weapon, not a bunker-buster. I meant my brother Atticus. He needs a place to work out and fight our own kind without ending up in rank fights. You guys could set up a hell of a training facility if you wanted to."

Axel's ice blue eyes got a faraway look, and he frowned and rubbed his jaw. "Maybe. Send Atticus over. We'll beat the shit out of him for you."

"Good." Benedict linked his arm with Eloise's and led her outside. No telling what went on in her head, if Val's daughter was the one who stole the money and betrayed her. He ached to embrace her, to hold her head to his shoulder and reassure her that everything would be fine. They stood next to the car as she stared into the city, every angle in her face hard and unyielding. He took a deep breath; she needed to do it for herself, or she would never conquer the monster part of

Chasing Trouble

herself she so feared. So he unlocked the car. "Where are we going now?"

"City General," she said, the words barely more than a hiss.

He didn't question her as she got in the car, nor did he say anything as they drove through the city to the massive hospital only a few blocks from work. An ambulance raced past them and careened into the emergency room entrance. Benedict parked and reached for her hand. "Eloise. Come back. What are you going to do?"

Only her profile was visible as she glared at the hospital. "I have to know if Cal was part of it. If he's faking."

"Cal wouldn't —" Benedict knew the heir to the jackal pack, and he was as straightforward as a scavenger could be.

"We'll find out." She shoved the door open and strode toward the hospital.

Benedict cursed under his breath, dialing Edgar as he jogged to catch up. "We're at the hospital. It was the hyenas."

A long pause, then Edgar exhaled. "So we're going to war with the hyenas?"

"Maybe not." But neither of them believed any doubt remained. He would never let Val Szdoka take advantage of Eloise or harm her in any way, and Val Szdoka would not take kindly to the Chase pride's interference. So war it might be. "But prep Logan. If he's not in, I'm still with her."

"You'd go against Logan's orders, if he told you to stay out of it." His older brother sounded pained. Benedict barely caught the receptionist telling Eloise Cal's room number, his fancy shoes slipping on the polished linoleum. Edgar pronounced each word precisely in the static of the phone. "You would leave the pride for her."

And for the first time in his life, Benedict didn't have to think twice about disobeying an order. "Absolutely. Shit, I gotta go."

He hung up and sprinted for the elevator, almost losing his hand in the doors as they closed. Eloise, standing inside, just watched him with a blank expression under her sunglasses and her supernatural hair hovering as she disappeared from his view. He took the stairs three at time but lost her on the fourth floor, phone clenched in his hand as he searched. The crashing sounds were a dead giveaway, though. When he skidded into the doorway of the luxury room, he found Eloise standing over Cal, beating his mottled chest with her fists.

A thin man lurched up from where his chair landed across the room and advanced on her, a knife in his hand, and Benedict growled. The man paused but didn't drop the knife, shooting Benedict a hateful look over his shoulder. "Have you come to finish him off?"

Eloise grabbed Cal's shoulders, trying to rouse him. "Stop faking it. Open your eyes. Open your eyes!"

The thin man, features almost identical to Cal's, bared his teeth with a keening sound. "He won't. He won't ever open his eyes."

"Liar," she snapped, turning to confront him. She ripped off her sunglasses. "He was in on it, he and Lacey decided —"

"Don't say that bitch's name in front of me!" The thin man lunged forward, knife ready, and Benedict jumped.

Cold blasted out of Eloise in a rolling wave, knocking Benedict back a step even with a glancing blow, and his limbs tingled. But the skinny dude, Cal's relative — he took the brunt of whatever it was she did. He froze, stuck to the floor.

And as Benedict stared at him and then Eloise as she struggled to breathe, realization dawned. A gorgon. "Medusa," he said. The numbness settled in his hands and a terrifying possibility seized his chest. "Did you just — is he petrified?"

Her mercury eyes lifted to his, and nothing registered in them. No fear, no remorse, no familiarity. Nothing. A chill shot down his spine and the world grew dark around the edges.

chapter 16

Everything in me turned to ice when I saw the photo of Lorraine and Heba. Not just some of Val's people gone rogue, but her daughter and niece. Lorraine would never cross her mother. Ever. She only obeyed. So if Lorraine was in on the scam, so was Val.

It seemed I blinked and then we were at the hospital, in a private room, and a man I remembered as Cal's brother threatened me. The monster mojo lashed out, silenced him. Silenced some of the pain of the morning. Betrayed. Twice betrayed.

And then Benedict, eyes wide as he edged away from me, said, "Medusa," as if somehow I'd betrayed him too.

Guilt crushed me and cold surged out, wanted to making everything in the world ice and stone so nothing else would warm my heart and blood and soul. Deaden feelings so I would never be hurt again. Benedict swayed back, and for the first time I saw real fear in his eyes. Even when he teased, I knew he didn't fear me. I knew he believed me better than I really was.

I missed that.

But first there was the matter of Cal Armstrong. I turned my attention to his brother, Harrison, and willed some of the ice into my words. "Start talking."

Only vile cursing spilled forth, until I said, "This will wear off and you'll be able to walk again. I can just as easily make it permanent."

"Fuck off," he spat. "He told me that bitch wanted to elope. She said to meet at Aaron's and they'd get money and a head-start. He asked me to drive him, drop him off. So one of the pack cars wouldn't be left on Evershaw's territory." His eyes rimmed with red and he looked away. "Four hyenas showed up. They grabbed him, dragged him away before I could help him. By the time I reached him, he looked like that," and the man jerked his chin at Cal, swollen and bloodied and bruised.

The ice made it difficult to swallow. I looked at Cal, counted the slow, uneven beeps of a heart monitor. "Why isn't he healing?"

"The bitch gave him something so he couldn't." Harrison snarled a terrible angry, grieving sound. "She wanted him to suffer. They left him to die in the cold on the wolves' territory."

"Is he —"

"Braindead," he said. Bitterness rolled off him and nearly knocked me back. "We're only waiting for the extended pack to arrive so we can bury him."

I looked at Cal and some of the ice around my eyes cracked. I'd liked him. A lot. He'd been nice to me when he didn't have to be, even when no one else was around. Warmth trickled down my cheek. "I'm sorry."

"Sorry doesn't avenge my brother." Harrison growled as he struggled to move, but his feet and legs remained stone.

"After you bury him," Benedict said, slow and careful. "Your people will go after the hyenas?"

"Wouldn't you?" The jackal gestured at his brother's broken body.

"I left the money at Aaron's," I said. The words felt heavy and slow, landing with greater weight than anything I'd ever said before. "Lacey asked me to set it up so she and Cal would have money to start their life together. The money disappeared. The hyenas took it, the same ones who murdered Cal. And now Val blames me. If I don't have the money and Lacey back to her tonight, I'll pay for both."

"My brother is dying." Harrison fixed me with a wintry look. "I don't give a fuck about your problems."

"You should," I said. "Because if Val set this up to kill me and split Cal and Lacey up, then she's probably ready for a war with the jackals and all of your people will end up right there," and I pointed at poor Cal. My voice shook as badly as my hand. "So get your shit together, Harrison. If Lacey was in on it too, I'm surprised you're not already dead. If we can't work together, at least help me."

The jackal bared his teeth at me and tensed, attention going to the open door and some of the curious nurses and passersby who peeked in. Benedict shut the door but gave me a look like maybe he wanted to be on the other side of it, too. My heart melted, sank the rest of the way to my feet. But the lawyer only said, "We should get going."

"Get out of here," Harrison said. "And if you see that bitch again, tell her I'm coming for her."

"Stay away from her." I backed away toward the door, wishing I could say good-bye to Cal without losing the rest of my composure. "If she was part of this, she's mine. If she wasn't — anyone who touches her will end up a statue in my garden."

My lungs seized up and all the air went out of the room as I shoved past Benedict and into the hall, past the crowd on onlookers and at least one concerned nurse, and headed for the stairwell. I made it down one flight before my legs gave out and I collapsed onto the stairs, all the feeling draining out of me. Maybe if I sat there long enough, Val wouldn't look for me. Cal would wake up. Lacey would call to say it was a fucked up joke. Everything would go back to normal. Benedict would forget about me and go back his rich brothers. I could go back to staying at Ruby's bar when I got evicted from my apartment for being late with the rent again.

I covered my face and tried to breathe.

Clothing rustled behind me and the tap-tap-tap of Benedict's expensive shoes interrupted my panic, and then the warm bulk of his body eased onto the stair next to me. Something deep inside me eased, uncoiled. The tension faded. Some of the cold rage even thawed to lukewarm disgruntlement, and suddenly the world didn't feel so hopeless. I took a deep breath.

"Eloise," he said, then paused. I braced for the bad news, the condemnation for what I'd done and the lawyer-ese to tell me to stay the hell away from his family. Instead, his arm looped around my shoulders and drew me close to his side. He sighed. His cheek rested against the top of my head, and the hair-snakes moved to twine around him. "I'm sorry."

"For what?" My voice cracked and I wiped at my cheeks, horrified to find tears.

"For a lot of things." Benedict rubbed my upper arm, both of us staring at the blank wall ahead of us. "That Cal is dying, that Val probably set you up, that your friend might have been part of it."

I turned my face away so he wouldn't see, and wondered where my sunglasses were.

His deep breath jostled me a little, even more as he pulled me close and kissed the top of my head. "And I'm sorry for what I said, and for stepping back. That wasn't right, and I didn't mean it."

Of course he did. They always did. I remained rigid, unbending, even as he tried to comfort me. Waiting for the cold and ice to return so I could paralyze him and get on with my miserable, monstery existence. But nothing happened except a crack in the ice, more thawing. He still made me feel better, even when I wanted to hate him. Even when it would have been easier to run away.

Benedict knocked some of my hair out of his face and tried to rest his forehead against mine. "So here's the plan, at least from where I sit. If we can get your freaking hair under control, we get out of here before the rest of the jackals show up. We get somewhere safe to rest and eat and decide how we're going to deal with Val. Then we walk into this thing with clear minds, and we make sure she never bothers you again."

My heartbeat echoed in my ears with a dull thumping, slow and distant. We. He said 'we.' Not 'you.' I blinked, searching for a response, but when nothing came to mind, I waited.

He scowled and pushed another braid off his cheek, beginning to bat them away like an overzealous cat. "My apartment isn't far from here. There's still another ten hours or so until we meet with Val, right? Let's go get some food."

"Why are you so nice to me?" The words slipped out even though I meant to thank him and say I didn't need any more help, that I would face Val alone even if it turned me to ice forever.

Benedict pushed to his feet and descended a few stairs, until we were face-to-face. His eyes locked with mine, and not even a hint of trepidation showed in his expression. As if he weren't staring a gorgon in the eyes. "A lot of reasons, Eloise, but mostly because you deserve for people to be nice to you. Isn't that enough?" He held out a hand to help me up.

I couldn't move. "Are you really going with me to see Val?"

"No," he said, and my heart sank. Until he bent down until we were nose-to-nose, and he breathed, "I'm going with you to scare the fucking life out of Val and her daughters, so none of them bother you ever again." His lips pressed to mine and his hand slid into my hair, the kiss deepening as a searing heat burned through the cold in my heart. My hands lifted and slid into his hair, drawing him closer as his tongue teased mine and my heart jumped. Heat sparked through every inch of me but collected low in my stomach. Benedict pulled away suddenly, so suddenly I gaped at him, mouth open and hungry for his. He tapped his chin. "Although I suppose we have to *see* Val in order to —"

"Someone's got jokes," I said under my breath as I shoved to my feet and tried to knock him down the rest of the stairs. My pulse raced in my ears and dizzy stars spotted my vision. "You're not as funny as —"

He gripped my waist with sudden force and lifted me, spun me, pinned me against the rough concrete wall. I gasped, searching his face for the threat, but Benedict's gold eyes devoured me and then his mouth did as well. He nipped my chin, behind my ear, down my throat until I slid boneless against the wall and would have fallen if not for his thigh, wedged between mine.

A deep rumble started in his chest, almost a purr, as his palm slid under my sweater and up my ribs. He kissed me hard, then broke contact to study me as my chest heaved. "I think I'm funny."

His fingers grazed a heated trail across my breasts, searching for my nipples under the sweater, and I made an indecent noise as I wriggled and tugged on his shirt. Benedict adjusted his leg, pressed between mine, and hiked me up higher on his thigh. "Don't you think I'm funny, Eloise?"

"F-funny," I gasped, head tilting back as he traced the waist of my jeans, played with the button and belt loops. I closed my eyes. "Funny isn't your gift."

"Oh," he said, all grumbly and deep. "Then what is my gift, babe?"

My insides clenched and I melted against him, holding on to his shoulders and using him as a furnace and a convenient wall. I wanted him naked, in a bed. With no expectations between us other than passion. Even if Val tried to kill me. I touched his face, searching those radiant golden eyes for a hint of our future. "Driving me to your apartment seems like a gift."

"That might be a place to find my gift," he said. Benedict took my earlobe in his teeth and nibbled, then muttered a curse and jerked back. I blinked, dazed with the thought of going back to his apartment and tangling our limbs together for the rest of the afternoon, and he scowled as he waved his hands around my head. "But first we're going to get your hair under control, because I want to taste every inch of your body and not have your braids get in the way."

Chasing Trouble

I smiled, trying to gather the hair back, but wasn't sure how to tell him the hair wasn't acting up because of the earlier threats and anger. No, the hair only got grabby when it found someone it liked. Someone we liked. Someone I really loved.

I might be in serious trouble, but so was he.

chapter 17

Benedict didn't say much in the car as they drove to his apartment, though he held Eloise's hand and took mental stock of all the tasks still waiting before they faced off with the hyenas. The first and most important was taking care of Eloise — feeding her, getting her to calm down and relax, and maybe sleep. So he walked her into the penthouse apartment in one of the high-rise apartment buildings in the heart of downtown and sat her down at his kitchen table. She watched him in silence, some of the apprehension back in her face.

He put a cup of coffee in front of her and poked her side. "Smile already. How's grilled cheese?"

Her nose wrinkled. "Grilled cheese?"

"It's my specialty." He tried to channel Natalia's wounded professional pride when someone challenged her cooking and arched his eyebrows. "You haven't lived until you've had my grilled cheese."

She still looked dubious, but she shrugged and concentrated on the coffee. "I guess we can always order in."

Benedict snorted. He needed to up his game. But grilled cheese was his default comfort food. When he was younger and Carter came home from school upset, grilled cheese was the only thing Benedict was allowed to make after a few near-misses with kitchen fires. So he made a sandwich for Carter and tried to talk him through whatever bullying or torment the other kids heaped on him. His younger brother refused to tell their parents or older brothers, assuming that the teasing would only get worse if he called in adults to help. So Benedict tried to look out for him and remain the shoulder to cry on. Grilled cheese always helped, and tomato soup in winter.

He stacked sharp cheddar, Gruyere, smoked bacon, and the last few slices of a rosemary ciabatta loaf he'd stolen from Natalia's kitchen on his counter. He waved a spatula over his shoulder at her as he bent to search for the single frying pan he owned. "Just wait. Your hair is going to go nuts over this."

That got a laugh at least, and something inside him eased. The flat expression and dead eyes when she faced him at the hospital still chilled him to his bones, and the devastation in her face when she realized he feared her hurt worse still. That she could laugh meant they could recover. They could rebuild. He hummed at he cooked, trying to disguise the purr that rattled through his chest as the lion luxuriated in the knowledge that she was safe in his den, he would feed her, and then he would take her to his bed for some fun. Then he would kill her enemies. A good day overall.

Benedict served her the first sandwich, golden and melty and smelling heavenly right out of the pan, and winked as he set it in front of her and snuck a kiss. He didn't even mind the strands of hair that tickled his throat. He minded even less as she took the first bite of the sandwich and what might have been a moan escaped. He just concentrated on the pan and his sandwich, sneaking a piece of the bacon before saying, "Was I right?"

"Maybe." The word barely snuck out as she chewed. "Is there enough bread for another one?"

"Of course." Benedict smiled, pleased that she would be well-fed. He slid his sandwich onto her plate from the pan and snuck another kiss. That one lingered and instead her hands caressed his shoulders and neck, holding him close. She tasted delicious. He broke away before he dropped the hot pan on either of them, but pecked her lips once more. "And enough for more if you want them. Always whatever you want, Eloise."

She smiled dreamily, palms sliding against his cheeks, and she rose from the table to kiss him. "I want you."

"Good." He growled more than he intended, imagination going into overdrive with his bedroom only steps away, but he held the lion back. "Finish your sandwich, and I'll eat my sandwich, and then ... then I get you for dessert."

Color suffused her cheeks and the hair started to float in a cloud around her. Her gray eyes turned more silver as her fingers trailed down his chest to rest on his belt buckle. "Sounds like a plan."

The effort to walk away and finish the sandwiches probably took a couple years off his life, but they both needed food. Fucking on every surface of his apartment could wait at least thirty minutes. He still barely waited for the cheese to melt before pronouncing his sandwich was done, and she still chewed her last bite as he threw her over his shoulder and marched into his bedroom.

Benedict tossed her onto the bed and pulled off her shoes and pants while she fought off the shirt and tossed it across the room. He stood back to take her in, the rise and fall of her perfect breasts and the round, welcoming curves of her hips and thighs. His dick had been hard for the last hour, at least, but the sight of her on his bed, reaching out to try to take off his pants, nearly pushed him over the edge.

But he pulled out the drawer of his bedside table before her touch became too distracting and held up a scrap of silky fabric. Her eyebrow arched and a smartass comment hovered on those lush lips, still red and bruised from kissing.

He beat her to it and kissed her again, then sat back. "Just so you don't blind me with those lasers of yours," he said, then tossed her the velvet sleep mask. "I don't want to be interrupted."

She laughed with a shiver of excitement running through the sound. "You're not serious."

"Very." He crawled up her body to straddle her hips and brace his hands by her shoulders. She shivered, staring up at him with smoldering heat. He kissed her and settled his weight on her hips, loving the warm comfort of her body. The give as he squeezed her thigh. He moved enough to put the mask on her, smiling as she went still. "Just relax."

"Easy for you to say," she said under her breath. "You're not facing a firing squad in six —"

"Nope." Benedict tugged on the mask and peeked underneath, made sure she could see his serious face. "We're not talking about six hours from now. We're here, now, in this bed. Together. That's all the matters. Right?"

For the first time, he saw fear in her eyes. But she nodded. "Right."

Layla Nash

"Good. Now stop interrupting me." He let the mask snap into place and slid back down her soft curves, running his hands over as much of her bare skin as he could manage. So soft and warm and smooth, smelling like cocoa butter and honey and lust. Her breasts tightened, peaked, as he teased. Her breath caught when he nibbled on her pink nipples, and her head fell back on the pillow. He knew the blindfold was a good idea.

Benedict hummed against the tender flesh in his mouth and she jumped, catching his shoulders. A purr ignited in his chest as he smelled her intensifying desire, and he continued to play with her breasts until her hips lifted against him, asking for more. She grabbed handfuls of the sheets and a low moan escaped as he slowed the torment, backed off, refocused on blazing a trail down to her pussy.

Eloise wiggled under him until Benedict pinned her hips down with one hand, the other pressing her thighs apart. Her head lifted in alarm as he breathed against her stomach. "What are you doing?"

"What do you think I'm doing?" He laughed, then blew a raspberry on her stomach. "I'm going to eat your pussy until you come all over my face, then I'm going to fuck you. Or you'll fuck me. Depends on how tired I am from all the pussy licking."

She covered her face with her hands, entire body shaking with what he hoped was laughter, then tried to push his head away. "Just fuck me already, I don't want to wait."

He studied the quickening of her breath, the tension in her legs against his shoulders. So he stroked her damp slit, already open to him, with the tip of his finger. Teasing more. Eloise cleared her throat, though her voice went high as he kissed the

Chasing Trouble

warm mound above her clit. "You don't really have to —" She trailed off into breathy moans as his tongue circled the heated pearl and Benedict pressed his middle finger into her channel.

God, she tasted amazing. Her thighs tightened against his ears but he didn't care. He would eat away all damn day if he could, especially with the sounds she made — all soft and needy. He backed off to nibble the insides of her thighs when Eloise's hips started moving. He wanted to draw it out as long as possible, to bring her to the edge again and again until she knew — would always remember — he was the one who made her come harder than she ever had before.

Her intoxicating scent swirled in his senses, invaded his brain, imprinted on his heart. His lion wanted her, wanted to mark her. Benedict bit her clit gently and she came off the bed with a cry, her entire body flushing from head to toe as she shook. He smiled against her flesh but didn't stop. A leisurely pace sucking and licking and nipping kept her on the edge after the first one. He worked two fingers into her as her muscles clenched, drawing him in.

Her hands gripped his hair as her head tossed on the pillow and her hips pushed up at his mouth, begging for more, and he only backed off again. She growled in frustration and tried to drag him on top of her. "Please. Come on. Please."

"Please what?" he murmured. He ran his tongue over and around her clit until every muscle in her body tightened and she answered only in incoherent mumbles. His dick was hard enough to break itself off, it felt like, and he wanted to be in her. He wanted to feel the ripples of her orgasm, wanted to know she fucked back at him when she raised her hips.

"Please," she said, half-moan. Sweat beaded on her upper lip and she squeezed her breasts before trying to pull him on top of her once more. "Benedict, please."

"Well, since you asked so nicely..." He moved up her and kissed her deeply, tasting her pussy and mouth at the same time, and his cock nudged between her legs.

She inhaled sharply. Her legs fell open and he groaned, easing the tip into her past the tight muscles of an aftershock. Eloise arched her back, tilted her hips, and he slid home. She encased him like a hot, wet glove, and every little ripple of her core tried to drag him to climax.

Benedict groaned a curse, resting his forehead against her shoulder. Heaven. Heaven was a pussy slick with desire, open and willing and moving to draw him in. He kissed her again, thrust as gently as he could to fill her. She winced a little, moving, and he started to withdraw. Disappointing, sure. He wanted to see her face as he fucked her. Wanted to hear every little sigh and gasp, wanted to see the sweat dripping down her face.

Eloise locked her legs around his waist. "Stay. Deeper."

"I'll hurt you," he said. He kissed her again, wanted to reassure her he wasn't disappointed, even if he was. "It's okay, we can —"

"I want you," she said, locking her arm around his neck. Her voice coming from behind the velvet eye-mask made it kinkier, somehow. But she wasn't letting go. "I want you in me. I want you to fuck me hard. *Hard.* I want to feel you."

He groaned at the dirty words, his hips jerking forward until his stomach pressed against hers and she tensed and cried out under him. She bucked, nails raking stinging furrows down his back. Benedict couldn't have stopped for anything in the world. He grabbed her hips and held her in place to receive him, pounding into her ample hips until he knew she bruised under his hold. Heard only the wet sounds of their mating and the slapping of flesh — his balls against her ass, over and over and over as he struggled for control and the lion roared to put her on her knees and fuck her from behind. Claim her.

Benedict pinned her shoulder down as Eloise writhed, and her pussy clenched around him like a velvet fist. She cried out and went still, the sound dying in her throat as her expression froze. He couldn't stop, pounded through the orgasm until she twitched with each drag of his body against her but he only caught her leg, pressed it up until her ankle braced on his shoulder and her body was truly his to plunder.

He snarled, lost control. He moved in abrupt, vicious thrusts, spreading her open and taking all of her. Her dark hair covered his pillows, her sweat soaked into his sheets. Blush stained her cheeks as she tossed and moved under his punishing rhythm, begging him. Begging him for what, he didn't know.

Pressure built in his balls as the orgasm approached like a freight train, and he snarled, slapped her hip hard enough to leave a mark. Fucked her until she wailed and went boneless in the sheets, until his entire fucking body seized up as he shot wave after wave of himself into her.

Eloise remained still except for her panting breath. Benedict released her leg and held his weight off her chest, waiting for his own breathing to slow. He removed the blindfold as he kissed her throat. "Good?"

She nodded with her eyes closed, a hint of a smile curving her lips, and he exhaled in relief. He hadn't meant to get so rough, but having her beg him, all soft and delicate and helpless, turned him into the lion in human form. Benedict lay next to her and traced a path around her breasts and stomach, inhaling the scent of her sweat and their intermingled fluids. He wanted to lick everything off her, roll around in her scent until she marked him as deeply as he'd marked her.

But there was still planning to do. Val Szdoka and her pack still waited for them in a few hours. Benedict kissed her forehead and drew the sheets up over her, murmuring, "I'll be back in a minute," before slipping out of bed.

He didn't bother with clothes as he found his cell phone and wandered through his living room. Edgar, as usual, was his first call. He answered but didn't speak. Benedict let the silence stretch, then took a deep breath. "What's the verdict?"

"You should call Logan."

"Ed —"

"Call Logan." And the line went dead.

Benedict rubbed his face, pacing another few minutes before daring to dial his oldest brother's number. When Logan answered, Benedict said, "Just listen. I —"

"You listen." Logan's voice was at least half growl. "Are you fucking kidding me? After everything we've accomplished here, everything we've built — you'd throw it away for this girl? A girl who stole your wallet, ditched you and took your clothes, and probably stole from Val Szdoka. And you want to go to war with the hyenas over her."

Benedict braced his free hand on the marble counter in his kitchen, bending forward to stare at the floor. He only had one answer. "Yes."

Chasing Trouble

"And if I ordered you to stay home, you would disobey. You would betray your family, your *brothers*, and your kind for this girl. You would turn your back on the life I built for us."

"Yes."

Cursing exploded on the other end of the phone, then grew muffled. An argument echoed and Benedict frowned, looking at his phone before holding it back to his ear. A heartbeat later, Natalia's cool voice reached him. "Benedict, do you love her?"

Still only one answer. "Yes."

"And does she love you?"

"I believe — yes. She does." He thought of her asleep in his bed, the way she'd kissed him in the stairwell and melted into his arms. The way her hair tried to grab him and drag him closer.

Natalia said something sharp to Logan, and Benedict knew he had a chance. She sounded unruffled, as if they discussed the weather. "Then we'll be there. Where and when?"

His heart soared. Thank God. They wouldn't have to do this alone. Eloise would know she joined a family, a pride that protected each other. He told Natalia the time and place, and she thanked him politely and berated Logan for being an unromantic dick before the line went dead.

Benedict made a mental note to get Natalia a hell of a Christmas present.

He wanted to crawl in next to Eloise but instead called Ruby and Rafe to explain the threat to their friend. The wolves remained noncommittal about joining a fight, but from the irritation in Ruby's voice, he knew they would contribute in some way. He even called Miles Evershaw to suggest he might be able to make a point to Val Szdoka about using his territory for some dirty business.

Layla Nash

Kaiser's phone rang several times before the bear picked up, sounding half asleep. "What's the news, Chase?"

Benedict debated only a moment before explaining the situation. The bears deserved a head's up in case Val had them on retainer. "I don't want you walking into something without knowing what it is. My brothers and I will be there to protect Eloise, and BloodMoon and SilverLine may also be in the area."

Kaiser made a deep humming noise in his chest. "That's good to know. I do not believe we will be nearby. Unless, of course, you need us to be."

"I won't ask you to start a feud with the hyenas, Kaiser. But Val Szdoka has been pitting both sides against the middle for too long. It's time the hyenas learned they aren't the king of this jungle."

The bear snorted. "True. We might be there. I cannot speak for the rest of the family. We have a great deal of work to do, turning the place into a gym. Thank you for the suggestion."

Benedict blinked. "You're welcome. Have a good one, Kaiser, and thanks for your help today."

"Not a problem." He yawned, then said, "You might talk to the coyotes and jackals. I know they were displeased with the hyenas earlier."

And the line cut off. Benedict paced through the kitchen as he searched for contacts in the other shifter communities. He wanted to bring every weapon to the fight again Val. He wouldn't fight fair. Eventually he called Atticus and asked him to reach out through some of the coyotes who worked the underground fights. He didn't want Harrison and the jackals up in arms about everyone, but knowing where they stood meant less worrying about wild cards in what would certainly be a tense standoff.

He slid back into bed next to her. She didn't wake but turned toward him, snuggled into his side and pressed her face against his shoulder. She sighed, content. Benedict lay awake, staring up at the ceiling. He would start a fucking war to keep her safe and next to him.

chapter 18

The pleasant ache in my abs reminded me of why I would fight to live, as did Benedict's hand playing with my fingers on the console between our seats in the SUV. Love, or at least the possibility of it, was worth fighting for.

He didn't speak after we got in the car, and in the silence, I reviewed every possible argument and threat and outcome. Maybe Val would come out swinging. Maybe she would stage an ambush after lulling me into a false sense of security. She preferred mental games, though. Maybe she would try to have me volunteer my way into servitude.

The car rolled to a stop a few blocks from the meeting place. Benedict turned off the car and braced his hands on the steering wheel. "Are you ready?"

"No." I took off my sunglasses and attempted a smile. "But that doesn't matter."

"You'll be fine." He touched the tip of my nose. "And don't be afraid to zap her with your freaky eyes, either. Petrify the shit out of her if you want. We'll be behind you."

"It's not my behind I'm worried about," I said with a laugh. "Her daughters will charge me from the front."

He pretended to examine my rear in the seat, frowning as he tugged on a belt loop of my jeans. "I'm very concerned about your behind, frankly. I might need to check it again. Just to make sure."

I swatted his hand away and opened the door. "Enough, I have to —"

He tugged my arm and pulled me back, across the console, and kissed me, tongue plunging into my mouth as I drew breath to tell him I loved him. Heat seared through me as his lips crushed mine and his hand slid into my hair, gripping the back of my head to hold me close. I touched his face, stubble on his cheeks rough against my palms, and thought about climbing over the console to straddle his lap. He broke the kiss but pressed his forehead to mine until our noses bumped.

He said very quietly, "I love you, Eloise Deacon. You are not a monster. You are strong and capable and worthy, and you have an ass that doesn't quit. All admirable traits. Do not ever forget that."

My throat closed around an emotion I didn't recognize, though my eyes burned with tears. I broke away before he noticed my reaction, instead saying over my shoulder, "My ass is pretty admirable," as I jumped out of the car and walked away.

But my hands shook as I approached the abandoned lot, overgrown with weeds and a couple of automotive skeletons, where Val wanted to meet. A single streetlamp provided just enough light to create some terrifying shadows. I didn't have to wait long. Val approached, several of her people with her in human and animal form. I held back my rage, let it simmer in my heart as I searched her expression for any hint of remorse. Any hint of humanity at all.

Val's eyes narrowed as she looked at me. "You don't have my money or my daughter. And yet you showed up. I don't know if you're brave or just stupid."

"Both, probably." The scary mojo worked up my spine in icy tendrils, just waiting for the opportunity. Cold gathered around my eyes as soon as I saw her face, heard the disregard in her voice. The thought of Benedict and his brothers, watching from the darkness around the pool of light where I stood, gave me the courage to say more. "But I could say the same about you."

She rocked back on her heels, laughing. "What, you took the money you stole from me and invested in some bodyguards? That makes you brave? Cut the shit, Eloise. Give me my money, tell me where Lacey is, and I'll probably let you live."

"Ask Lorraine." My hands clenched into fists at my sides. I recognized one of the hyenas as Lorraine, but Heba stood in human form at Val's shoulder. "Or Heba there. Ask them where your money is. If you don't already know, that is."

A twitch of doubt made Val frown. Her upper lip curled in a snarl. "I don't like what you're implying, Eloise."

I forced a laugh through the terror and anger clogging my throat. "Implying? Please. I'll spell it out for you. Lorraine and Heba set this up, and maybe Lacey, too. They stole your money, they *killed* Cal Armstrong, and they're trying to set me up too. Well, I'm not going down without a fight."

Val's eyes went flat, emotionless. The vertebrae in her neck cracked as she rotated her head. She didn't take her eyes off me but snapped her fingers, her voice deceptively quiet. "Heba. Start talking."

The woman edged forward, glaring at me as she pulled her dark hair out of the way. "She's making shit up, highest. We didn't —"

"You're lying." The hyena queen's breathe rasped in her throat. "Tell me where Lacey is. Right. Now."

Heba swallowed as the hyena with Lorraine's coloring stalked from the darkness and fixed her with a yellow gaze. "She's chained up there," and Heba jerked her chin at a nearby abandoned building.

Val gestured and three of her people raced off into the night. The hyena queen still hadn't looked away from me, and the direct threat in her gaze set my heart racing and the ice coalescing in my head. When she went on, the blood froze in my veins as well. "We have a different problem now, Eloise. You've witnessed too much. You've seen Lorraine's disrespect, and Heba's disobedience. I should kill them for it, but I still have a use for them. You, on the other hand..." She shook her head, as if she regretted an unpleasant task. "Your utility has expired."

I drew breath to scream for Benedict as my hair flared out in a cloud and one of the hyenas barked a warning, and Val said, "Lorraine, go."

The growling mass of yellow and black fur leapt at me and I kicked, trying to keep her claws from me, but Lorraine's teeth sunk into my arm and wrenched. Flesh parted and an awful roaring filled the night. The pain of the bite sent cold through every part of me and I looked at Heba, watched unfeeling as she turned the blue-gray of new concrete. Frozen forever.

Something landed on the hyena, still chewing on me, and that freed me up to lurch toward Val, arms outstretched. She would pay. I would be free of her forever, and the pain in my head would fade eventually. The cold burst in my eyes, filled the world with ice and rage and power, and I saw the fear in her eyes. Saw the horror in her expression, the way her fingers shook as she held up — a mirror.

A mirror.

And then it was my own face, devoid of emotion and framed by a cloud of black hair, staring at me. The cold snapped back, hit me in the gut, and everything stopped. Feeling disappeared, I couldn't blink, nothing worked. I felt as if I were falling but nothing else moved, and I tried to scream.

I tried to scream.

No sound escaped. A lion flew through the air in my peripheral vision and then Benedict's face appeared in front of me. Mouth open as he yelled, eyes wide and molten gold. *I love you* I tried to say, but not even my lips would move.

Everything went dark.

chapter 19

Benedict saw her freeze. He saw the mirror the hyena queen held and terror seized his lungs. Knocked the breath from him until he couldn't feel his hands and his vision spotted with dark blotches. His legs moved before he thought, even as Edgar tried to grab his arm and hold him back, but he had to save Eloise. Had to protect her as that fucking hyena tried to tear out her throat.

Ruby, Rafe, and a dozen other wolves descended on the hyena, driving it away and killing it in the dark, and a sleek lion with a peach fuzz mane crashed into Val Szdoka with a roar that shook his bones. Carter. Thank God for Carter.

But Benedict crouched by Eloise, patting her face. Yelling her name. Begging her to stay.

She just stared straight ahead, frozen. Frozen. Cool to the touch, a grainy texture to her skin. Like stone.

He snarled, roared his pain to the moon, and the wolves howled in response. The eerie sound floated into the night and set the hair on the back of his neck on end. His vision blurred and Benedict thumped Eloise's chest. "Damn it. Damn it. Wake up. *Look at me.*"

Nothing. Not even a blink. Her hair didn't reach for him, just lay in stiff cords like a starfish around her head. He pulled her into his lap, didn't care that the blood from her injured arm coated his clothes. He stared around into the darkness. The sounds of conflict rose, no doubt his brothers taking care of the rest of Val's people, but that didn't help Eloise. Didn't bring her back. He rocked her. "A doctor. Please, I need a doctor. Anyone. *Someone.*"

An eternity passed before a pair of bare feet shuffled into his field of vision, and Benedict looked up. Owen, the sleepy-eyed black bear from Kaiser's group, stood next to him, wearing only gym shorts. "I was a Navy Corpsman. Medic. Let me look at her."

Benedict stared at him, unwilling to release her. Guarding her.

Kaiser approached from the darkness. His voice was even, kind. "He might be able to help, Ben. Put the girl down."

His arms didn't work well, jerky and uncoordinated so he almost dropped her onto the broken concrete lot. Owen crouched next to her, quickly arranging her head and limbs to evaluate pulse and respiration and circulation as Benedict held his breath and didn't dare to hope. She looked so pale and cold. Vacant. Like an empty husk. The breath caught in his throat, too close to a cry.

Carter, still in lion form, stalked up and head-butted him, his muzzle coated with blood. Benedict barely noticed, looping his arm over Carter's shoulders so he wouldn't fall apart completely. She had to live. She had to.

He should have made her stay away from the meeting with Val. He'd wanted to go alone, but she argued. Said she had to take care of her own business, clean up her own messes. He should have locked her in the apartment to keep her safe. He couldn't swallow as grief welled up.

Owen anchored his fingers to her throat, searching for a pulse, and looked at Benedict. "What is she?"

"G-gorgon," he said, though the word caught in his throat and all he could think of was when he backed away from her at the hospital, when he feared her. The look in her eyes when she knew it... He grabbed handfuls of his own hair, wanting to tear his head apart. "She's part medusa."

"That explains it." Owen studied her arm, then bent to hover his cheek over her mouth. Checking for breath. He ran his knuckles across her sternum with enough force Benedict lurched forward to kill him for hurting her, but Eloise barely twitched. The bear's expression grew more guarded, less optimistic.

Benedict held his breath, staring at her chest so hard a white hot pain ignited behind his eyes. She had to be okay.

Owen sighed, sitting back on his heels. "I don't know much about gorgons, Ben. I think she's still alive. Thought I felt a pulse, but it's slow, sluggish."

"Will she wake up?" The words barely escaped in a whisper, and Carter grumbled his support, one massive paw landing on Benedict's leg.

"Depends on if her peepers were set to stun," Owen said, then held up his hands as the lion snarled. "I'm serious. She's not as bad as that chick," and he pointed at the statue that Eloise called 'Heba.' "So clearly something was different. Harrison said she paralyzed him at the hospital, right? Maybe it was that. Or maybe the mirror dilutes the effectiveness. There's no telling right now."

Benedict shook his head, kept shaking it, but nothing else would work. Eloise. His lion roared, raged. Cried out for her.

Edgar appeared from the shadows, wiping blood off his hands, and took in the scene with a grim expression. "Where to now, Owen? Hospital?"

"I don't think the humans are ready for this," the bear said. He frowned and picked up some of her hair, then shook his head. "There's another option, a makeshift place we use when someone is injured. We took Cal there at first, before it became clear he ... wouldn't wake up. It's not up to the Chase brothers standard of luxury, but it should be enough to get her through the next day or two."

"I've never heard of it," Edgar said.

"Believe it or not, but a lot goes on in this city that isn't on your radar." Kaiser folded his arms over his chest, frowning down at Eloise. "We can talk more about that later. Owen, get her stable and take her to the field hospital. I'll bring her mate."

Benedict lurched to his feet as Owen and another bear put Eloise on a stretcher and lifted her. Carter nudged him back but Benedict tried to reach her. Tried to touch her again, even though the chilly texture of her skin gave him the shivers. She would get better. She had to get better. He couldn't live without her.

Kaiser steered him toward a car, shoved him in the backseat, and let Edgar get in the front. Benedict kept his eyes on the car where they loaded Eloise and drove into the night, bumping across the broken ground, and he clenched his hands on his knees. *Eloise. Fight. Fight to live.*

Chasing Trouble

Every chair in the room was uncomfortable. Benedict tried every one of them, over and over, hoping for something that wouldn't feel like a torture device. After three days at the hospital, praying Eloise would open her eyes, any chair would have felt like something out of the Inquisition.

Looking at her unmoving face, seeing her vacant eyes — that hurt worse than any physical pain.

Edgar sat near the grimy window, watching him watch Eloise. Benedict knew perfectly well why Logan sent Edgar to babysit him — to make sure Benedict didn't lose his shit if Eloise died, and to put Benedict down if he went rogue. There was no other explanation for Edgar being there.

They remained at the makeshift hospital, which was actually nicer than Benedict expected, because all the staff were shifters or nonhuman of some kind. They didn't ask questions about what she was, although the doctors hemmed and hawed over what could cause that kind of paralysis. They ran test after test after test, and yet found no answers. She wasn't fully stone, but she didn't wake. Didn't blink. Didn't eat or drink. Didn't seem to breathe.

His throat closed if he thought about it too much, so he pushed it away. Got up to pace again before settling on another chair. Rested his elbows on the mattress next to her side and stared at her. Willed her to blink and sit up and laugh at him.

Someone knocked but he didn't move. Edgar got up, nodding gravely as he shook someone's hand. "Harrison. I heard about Cal. Damn shame."

Benedict looked away from Eloise long enough to see Harrison Armstrong, the new heir to the jackal clan, standing in the doorway with a bouquet of flowers. He edged inside and set the flowers on a side table. "Thank you, Edgar."

Dark bruises marked Harrison's eyes, and a purple knot decorated his chin. He stood at the foot of Eloise's bed and studied her. "My brother passed yesterday. The funeral is this weekend. It would be best if the lions did not roam south of the city until Tuesday. While I understand the role Eloise played in discovering who killed Cal, the rest of the clan is not quite to that point."

"Understood," Edgar said. "Thank you for the notice."

The jackal took a deep breath. "And we owe you thanks as well, for allowing us to get a little vengeance for Cal during the confrontation with the hyenas. While I would have liked to kill Val Szdoka myself, that a lion did was sufficient."

"You did okay for yourself," Edgar said, then nodded at the other man. "Since you killed a hyena with your bare hands."

Harrison winced a smile. "Doesn't help any, though." He took a deep breath. "They said she's still stunned. Hasn't woken up yet."

"She will." Benedict rested his chin on the mattress next to her cool hand, playing with her fingers. "She'll wake up."

A long silence behind him, and Benedict wanted to turn and scream at both of them. Doubters. That negativity was why Eloise still slept. He couldn't stand the pity in Edgar's eyes when his brother tried to convince him to go home and sleep or shower or eat. Bullshit. Edgar just wanted to distract him so they could make Eloise disappear. Take her away from him. A growl rumbled in his chest at the thought.

Harrison cleared his throat. "I know where you're at, Benedict. I was there with Cal. I hope she gets better, man, but hope is a dangerous thing. Just — try to tell yourself she might not wake up."

"She'll wake up."

There wasn't any question. Benedict couldn't imagine any other future. She would get better, they would get married and have babies and life would be perfect. His eyes burned and he blinked rapidly to get rid of some moisture so he could see her face again.

The jackal retreated, headed for the door. "I'm sure she will. I'll see you at the council meeting next week, Edgar."

The door shut behind him but Benedict didn't move.

Edgar sat forward, elbows on his knees, and tried to get Benedict's attention. "Ben, you have got to go home. It's been three days. You need to sleep. Shower. Change your clothes. Get some food. Rest. Then you can come back. She'll be fine. We'll stay here with her."

"No." Benedict touched her hand again.

His brother sighed, then shoved to his feet. "Okay. Carter is on his way to sit with you. He's bringing food. If you don't eat something, I'll send Natalia over to force feed you. Got it?"

Benedict didn't blink or acknowledge his brother leaving. He couldn't look away from Eloise. Just in case she opened her eyes. He wanted her to see him when she woke up. Wanted her to know how much he loved her.

chapter 20

He didn't know how many days passed before Owen returned, but from the beard on his jaw, it was at least a week since Eloise entered the hospital. The bear walked in alone and handed Benedict a bag laden with what smelled like cheeseburgers. "Eat something, man. If she wakes up now, she'll take one look at you and start running."

A clawing hunger ignited in his stomach at the smell of the grilled meat. He reluctantly gave up his place next to her bed so that Owen could begin checking her vitals. As he mowed into the third cheeseburger, juice running down his hand and arm, Owen glanced back at him. "I read up on gorgons a bit. Thought there might be something to help, some legend about waking up from the medusa's gaze."

Benedict sat forward, heart leaping into his throat. "And?"

"Nothing about unfreezing victims, from what I found." Owen picked up her arm, his fingers against the pulse spot of her bruised wrist, and looked at his watch to count. After a long moment, he shook his head and replaced her arm on the mattress. Then he looked at Benedict, arms folded over his chest. "But there's another myth. No idea if it will work, man. Apparently the blood from the medusa's left vein is poison, but the blood from the right vein is healing. I don't put stock in magical fixes, but it seems like the only way to resurrect a medusa might be hidden in her blood. Maybe."

Benedict felt hope — real hope — stir in his chest since he saw her freeze that night so long ago. A chance. A real chance to wake her up.

Owen raised his hands to hold off Benedict's blazing eagerness. "If that doesn't work, there's one other option. I'll just say it now so you have the chance to mull it over. But I've gotta say, I don't think there's a real chance with that one. You could bite her, Benedict, and turn her. The healing properties of the shifter virus might save her, might push her through whatever this is. If Harrison recovered from it, maybe she could too. But then again, the hyena didn't."

He shrugged, tossing the dark hair out of his eyes. "Of course, Eloise seems like a strong-minded girl and I don't know if I'd want to be the guy who turned her into a shape-shifter without her permission. But that's me."

Benedict swallowed hard, the empty bag falling in tatters on the floor as he stared at her blank face. Would he change her in order to keep her? She might hate him forever if she woke up a lion, even more of a monster, and not by her choice. He shook his head and pushed to his feet, wiping his hands on the tail of his already ruined shirt. "The blood. Try the blood."

"Roger dodger," Owen said under his breath. He fussed with the tubes already in her, then held a small tray under a valve until rich crimson filled it.

Layla Nash

"How much do you need?"

"I have no idea," the bear said. He gave Benedict a sideways look before cutting off the flow and redoing whatever he'd undone. "Do I look like I've used gorgon blood before? I'm guessing as much as you are, Benedict."

Benedict nodded and tried to speak through a dry mouth. "Thank you."

"Don't thank me until she's up and about." Owen frowned at her, the small tray in his hand, then shrugged and used his fingers to smear some across her forehead. "I guess start with external application and hope that works?"

Benedict paced along the far side of the room to give Owen room to work while his lion snarled and fretted over another man touching her. The bear wiped the blood over her eyes, along her cheeks, then lips, and spread some along her throat. He focused on the pulse points and then in lines across her clavicle. He looked at Benedict, said, "I'll put some over her heart, but just want to make sure you know I'm not going for her tits, okay?"

He nodded, though he chewed the inside of his cheek ragged to keep from killing the kid as he moved the sheet back from Eloise and spread blood around her ribs and heart, under and over her perfect breasts. Then he covered her back up and wiped his hands off, frowning down at the red-smeared figure in the bed.

Benedict trusted himself to approach, breathing through his nose to get the scent of her in his brain, and held loosely to her ankle. Needing to touch her, to feel her skin for any hint that it warmed. Any hint that she woke.

Owen gestured at Eloise. "Try to wake her up."

His throat didn't work at first; he had to swallow several times before he managed to speak. "Eloise, wake up. Please. Come back."

Nothing. Benedict took a deep breath and rearranged her hair on the pillow. Bent close so only she would hear and the damn bear would not. "Please, baby. Please wake up. I need you."

He thought her skin felt less waxy, warmer to the touch, and some color grew in her cheeks. But when he looked up, Owen's expression remained doubtful. Benedict closed his eyes. This had to work. It had to work. He leaned and pressed his lips against her, tasting her blood but not caring. She didn't kiss him back.

He sat heavily in his chair. It felt like someone just punched him in the heart. She didn't respond. There was no change to her temperature, no hint she was any different than when Owen suggested using the blood. He covered his face and prayed the bear would leave before Benedict lost his composure entirely.

Owen sighed. "I'll keep searching, Benedict. If there's more than one of her out there, someone must know something about how to fix this. Just — keep trying to wake her up. Bring her back. Give her a reason to hold on and come back."

He patted Benedict on the shoulder and left, closing the door quietly behind him. Benedict waited a few moments so the shifter's superior hearing wouldn't be able to pick up on it, then let the despair wash over him. She wasn't coming back.

He begged her. Told her how much he needed her. Promised her the world and more. And in the end he knew Harrison was right — hope was a dangerous thing.

chapter 2 1

Everything felt dark and cold and close. Paralyzing. I couldn't move, couldn't get a good breath, couldn't open my eyes or focus. It felt like swimming up through lake water, so deep I couldn't see the light at the surface and just had to hope it was the right way. I heard Benedict in snippets, and wanted to cry as I heard the defeat and despair in his voice.

It went on forever, until I gave up hope of ever seeing him again, of ever holding him again, of hearing his laugh. And then — something changed. A familiar smell, husky and strong like the forest, reminded me of Kaiser's gym. Warmth spread across my forehead and then my cheeks and lips and eyes, seeping into me. More heat gathered down my throat and across my chest, until I felt my heart stir. Beat again. Thump with strength. And again, stronger. Faster. Better.

My mouth wouldn't work or I would have kissed Benedict back. I knew it was him even without the benefit of sight, I could taste him and knew he was still there. I tried to lift my arms, to pull him close as he begged me to come back, and I wanted to feel the searing heat of tears escape my eyes again when he held me close and told me how much he needed me.

But when he held my hand, I felt it. The warmth eased from where his fingers tangled with mine and up my arm, soaring into my chest until my lungs opened and I drew in the first deep breath of clean air. And promptly grimaced. He smelled *terrible*.

My eyes drifted open some time later after I drifted half-in the dark water, and I found darkness around me still. Night. A lamp cast soft shadows across the room, though, and when I focused, I could make out various shapes in the room. A few lived-in chairs, a table near the door, medical equipment, and the hospital bed where I lay. But the most important shape turned out to be right next to me — Benedict, sound asleep in a chair with his head pillowed on the mattress next to my hip. Snoring softly, his expression twitching in his dreams, he made my throat close and tears well up in my eyes.

The dreadful fear of the confrontation with Val, the hopelessness as I saw my face in the mirror — all of it drifted away to know that he stayed with me. And it must have been a while, because he had a full beard and smelled like a locker-room. But he was mine. I concentrated and managed to lift my hand, rest it on the back of his head, ease my fingers into his hair. Just wanting to feel him, to touch him.

I enjoyed the silence and the closeness, the sense that I was the only person in the world who saw him so vulnerable. He stirred, though, and my heart leapt to see his face. He blinked, then captured my hand in his.

"Hi," I managed to croak, my voice rusty from disuse and God only knows what. Screaming, maybe. The scary mojo paralyzing my vocal cords. I pushed away the thought.

"Hi," he said, sounding dazed. Benedict pressed my palm to his cheek, staring at me as if he'd never seen me before. "Is this is a dream?"

"I hope not," I whispered. The possibility that I would wake and be once more in that deep water shook me to my core, and I struggled to breathe.

"If it is," he said, grip tightening on my hand and knee. "We'll make the most of it. I thought I lost you, Eloise. I thought I would never find you again. I've never been so afraid of anything in my life."

"I missed you." I studied his face, intent on learning very line and scar and dimple in case I never got to see him again. "I could hear you but I missed you so much I couldn't breathe. Don't ever leave me again."

"Never." He caught my face, rising from the chair to kiss me. His lips burned against mine and ignited more warmth, spreading through the rest of me until I breathed easier still. It couldn't be a dream, it had to be real. He had to be real to make my blood race like that.

Benedict sat back but continued touching me anywhere he could find, running his thumb over my cheek again and again in a soothing gesture I leaned into. Loved. Would have purred if I could have. And for a first time, a hint of a smile touched his face.

I took a deep breath, unable to take my eyes off him. "What happened?"

"Lorraine wanted to take over after Val, so she tried to get rid of Lacey. We found Lacey — she's banged up and still healing, but she'll live. BloodMoon claims the kill with Lorraine, and SilverLine claims another hyena kill, someone who attacked them from the shadows. You got Heba, and Carter got Val." He eased closer, bumping into the mattress as if he wanted to move right through it to be closer to me. "Lacey took over the hyena family. The jackals served the hyenas with a blood debt for Cal's death, but waived it because the perpetrators were already killed. Harrison wanted to thank you for what you did to find out who was behind all of it. They're grateful."

My lips trembled as I struggled for control through the awful memories of the fight, being attacked by Lorraine, watching Benedict shout at me to come back... He made a pained sound and stood, drawing me into an embrace and rubbing my back as he made hush noises. "It's okay, Eloise. It's okay. I'm here."

The tears came harder and I shook with the effort of keeping back the ugly cry. It was bad enough my hair was gross and I smelled and he smelled, but the snot and blotchy face of an ugly cry was just too much. He made that grumbly lion noise and then was in bed with me, holding me tightly to his chest as he kissed all over my face.

He talked faster as I tried to breathe, and he paused only to kiss me more. "You're free of them, Eloise. They won't bother you anymore. It's all over. And it's a good thing, what happened. Val had a lot of dirt on everyone and was scamming pretty much every shifter group in the city. When we all came together to help you and find Lacey, the depth of her deceit was revealed."

I sniffled and blinked up at him. "Really?"

"Yes, really." He almost blinded me with his smile. "The pride and the packs and the bears and jackals and maybe even the hyenas are getting together, along with the loners, to form a council. An informal alliance. They want a way to deconflict when things like this come up. So instead of the jackals having to confront Val alone, the council will discuss matters and come to a consensus. An attack against one is an attack against all."

I pressed my face against his chest, despite a cheeseburger-scented crusty patch on his shirt, and draped my arm over his side so I could feel his heart beating. "That's a good thing."

"A very good thing," he murmured, kissing the top of my head. "It's an amazing thing. And I'm so glad you're here for me to tell you about it. Baby, you did so well. You were so brave and strong and powerful. You stood up to her and you didn't flinch."

Fatigue rolled over me but from his body heat and the steady thump-thump-thump of his heart, the deep rise and fall of his breathing, and not from deep water. I nuzzled closer to him, sighing. "Tell me more."

"About the council?"

"About anything." My arms tightened around him and I wiggled closer. "I need to hear your voice. In case I wake up and this is a dream, I want to remember the way you sound."

His voice held a roughness to it as he went on, stroking my hair as he held me closer and moved his leg over mine. "Well, Kaiser and the bears are a big part of it, but they're starting a gym for mixed martial arts and shifters. That could be a complete disaster, if only …"

He went on and I drifted, warm and content and safe. *Safe.*

Chasing Trouble

When I woke, the room filled with light and sound and sensations so strong I nearly cringed. Everything rushed in at once, but I was alone in the bed. A woman stood next to it, running a comb through my hair, and a giant of a man sat near the window with a frown on his face. The woman spoke first, smiling at me as she continued combing. "There you are. We sent Benedict home to take a shower and get new clothes — he was pretty ripe."

"Thank you," I said, and she smiled more. Her name came back slowly — Natalia, the charity lady. And the brute was Logan, her fiancé. Benedict's brother. "When is he coming back?"

"Soon." She started braiding my hair, fingers deft with multiple plaits starting at my hairline and working back in what felt like a complex pattern. "I wanted to wash your hair, babe, but didn't want to get you soaking wet. So that can wait a little bit. We'll be able to take you home tomorrow, from what the doctors said."

"Oh." I sighed. Wonderful. Home with Benedict. That sounded like perfection.

"Before Natalia starts painting a bedroom for you," Logan started, shooting the woman a dark look. She stuck her tongue out at him. He pretended not to notice, intense gaze on me. "We have some ground rules to establish."

I tensed, already bristling. "You won't keep me from Benedict."

A hint of white teeth shone in his mouth as his upper lip curled. "Don't try to give orders just yet, girl. Hear me out. I've never seen my brother like this before. He did not shower or shave or eat for over a week because he sat here, staring at you and begging you to wake up. I do not want to see him like that ever again, and I do not want to see what happens if you change your mind and decide to run away."

"I won't." I stared at my feet, hidden under the sheets, and wished Benedict were beside me instead of his douche-y older brother.

"Good." Logan's scowl deepened, though, and there wasn't a welcoming smile or any hint he actually thought it was good. "But I have to protect my family, and that means managing risk when we invite newcomers to join us. We will welcome you as a Chase on one condition — no more illegal shit. Edgar showed me some of your arrest records, and we will not tolerate —"

"Logan," Natalia said, and gave him a thin-lipped look that stopped him in mid-sentence. "Do not raise your voice."

I started to think I loved her. She was definitely my new hero.

And she made me brave enough to say, "I don't like doing illegal things. I don't. But I'm not going to sit around and let Benedict pay for everything. I've always had a job, even if those weren't the kinds of jobs you approve of. I'm not taking charity anymore. I have to work."

He scowled, leaning forward. "It isn't —"

"It's fine, babe." Natalia smiled at me as she tugged on the braids. "We have a couple of options. We weren't sure how you would be feeling, or what kind of stress you want to deal with, so there are several different choices. The bears are opening an MMA gym for shifters, to train and spar and do all sorts of manly things. Kaiser asked if you might be willing to work there part-time as a receptionist and as — insurance? Rumors got around about you being scary as hell when you're pissed off, *and* that you scared Axel into backing down, so Kaiser wants to take advantage of that to keep everyone in line as they're getting the gym off the ground."

I frowned, trying to remember what happened with the bears. Most of it was a blur. "I didn't scare Axel, he just —"

"You scared him," Logan said, gruff and pouting against the wall.

"Oh." A flush climbed my cheeks and I reveled in the feeling, wanted to proclaim the miracle to them. I felt warm. Flushed. A miracle. "I didn't mean to."

"It's a good thing." Natalia finished with my hair and took a step back, examining the results with a critical eye. Then she sat on the foot of my bed, patting my calf. "So that's one option, but if you don't want to deal with a sweaty gym and a bunch of asshole shifters all day long, you can come work at my restaurant. We can start you washing dishes — it's low threat but it's a lot of work. You can move up from there if you're interested in working in the kitchen, or we can move you to hostess or bread girl or something like that. Lots of options, honey."

Gratitude clogged my throat, but I managed to force "Thank you" past the knot.

She smiled, then gave Logan a sharp sideways look. "And if neither of those appeal to you, Eloise, we'll find something else. Right, Logan?"

He made a face, on the verge of a snarl, but eventually nodded. His eyes swirled gold and brown, and there might have been kindness mixed in with the worry and irritation. "Yes. We will find something *legal* for you to do."

I rested my head on the pillow, exhausted from holding it up so Natalia could braid, and desperately wanted to go back to sleep. It felt like my heart was out of shape and tired too soon. "If you're so concerned about legality, you might want to talk to Atticus. He makes a lot of money fighting, but I'm guessing he doesn't pay his taxes."

Logan face went red and he lurched to his feet. "What?"

I made a mental apology to Atticus and sank deeper in the sheets. Before I could speak, though, someone knocked on the door, and my heart stopped once more. Lacey, looking battered and bruised, stood uncertainly in the doorway. Natalia took one look at me and held out her hand to Logan. "Buy me dinner, babe."

The lion looked like he wanted to object, but he loved her so damn much he just took her hand and nodded a good-bye to me. They paused near the door and Logan nodded to Lacey as well. "Lacey. Congratulations on taking over the hyena clan. Let me know if you want to sit with the council."

"We're still recovering." Pain filtered across her face. "But thank you. We appreciate the opportunity to join."

Logan glanced back at me, irritation in every line of his expression. "I'm sure Benedict will be back soon. Try to stay awake so he doesn't berate me for wearing you out."

Natalia poked him in the ribs and waved to me, dragging the grouchy lion into the hall. Lacey watched them go, then eased into the room. "Hey."

I sat up and held out my hands, felt my face crumpling as tears burned my sinuses. "I was so worried about you. I couldn't find you."

"Oh my God, El, I thought they killed you too," and she lurched forward and threw herself into my arms. She crushed me to her, almost hyperventilating. "Lorraine kept saying these awful things she would do to you, I thought she would —"

"I'm so sorry about Cal," I whispered, unable to take it. "I tried to help him, I thought —"

We ran over each other, crying and asking forgiveness and being miserable together until I managed to sit back, wiping desperately at my cheeks as she did the same. She started to tell me about being the new queen hyena and whipping the family into shape, cleaning up the family business to get out of some of the illegal activities, but got only part of the way into it when someone cleared their throat at the door.

I looked up and saw Benedict, freshly shaven and wearing clean clothes and carrying a beautiful bouquet of roses. And a bag with what smelled like fried chicken. My stomach growled. "Hey."

"Sorry to interrupt." But he didn't look sorry, unable to take his eyes off me. "I like your hair."

"Thanks." I squeezed Lacey's hand. "This is Lacey. Lacey, this is Benedict."

"Benedict Chase," she said, getting slowly to her feet. "I've heard a lot about you. Thank you for helping Eloise."

"Not needed," he said, but shook her hand gently when she offered it. "We're glad you're well. Or at least getting there."

She laughed a little self-consciously and waved at her face. "Yeah. Taking longer than normal. They gave me something to keep me from shifting or healing, so it's been a slow road. I should be going. Just wanted to see for myself that you're awake." She crushed me in another hug and murmured, "He's cute. Good job."

I laughed a little as she untangled herself, and wiped my cheeks again. "Right. Can we get together soon? Lunch or something?"

"Always. Just text me when you're ready." She hugged me again, quick, and retreated, disappearing out the door without another word or a backward glance. My chest tightened. It wasn't fair. She didn't want to be queen of the hyenas; that was why she and Cal planned to elope. And with her sister's treachery and her mother's death, there it was. The rest of her life, decided for her.

I stared at where she'd gone as Benedict set the roses and the chicken on the slidey tray that fit over my hospital bed. "Do you think — could she abdicate? Let someone else be queen?"

He made a thoughtful noise, searching for the water pitcher and cups, and dragged the most comfortable chair closer to the bed. "Maybe. But the hyenas don't make it a habit of training more than one leader. I don't think there's anyone capable of leading the hyena family except her. It would take a while, but I'm guessing she could probably do it. Although..." He shook his head and cut off.

"Say it."

He sighed, collapsing into the chair and propping his shiny, expensive shoes up on the mattress near my knees. "Since she lost Cal, the extra work might be helpful to keep her mind off things. Keep her busy until she processes what happened."

"She lost a lot," I said and felt my throat close once more. I wanted to throw something across the room. Apparently being paralyzed by a medusa and then thawed meant your emotions wouldn't stay level at all. I put a hand to my forehead and struggled for control — if I started crying, Benedict would be in bed with me in a heartbeat. And I wanted to eat that chicken. "She'll be okay."

"She will," he agreed. He slid a plate and the tray over my lap. "Eat, woman. You're too thin. Natalia made this for you. If we don't eat every bite, she'll beat me. She's mean, that one."

I smiled and reached for a drumstick. Ridiculous men. I needed to have a heart-to-heart with Natalia sooner rather than later. I ate until my jaw ached, then lay back to watch Benedict finish off the remaining chicken with gusto. As I studied his profile, I said, "I want to go home."

"Tomorrow morning," he said, leaning to kiss me with chicken-flavored lips. "I am taking you home."

"Good." I sighed and relaxed against the bed, my eyes settling closed as fatigue washed over me once more. "Logan kept me up and really tired me out with all his questions. He was relentless."

A low growl rumbled from Benedict and I hid a smile. I owed Logan a little bit of trouble.

chapter 23

Darkness washed over me, cold covered every inch of me, and I struggled to breathe. Nothing moved. Paralyzed. Blind. Deaf. So very cold.

I sat straight up, sucking in great lungfuls of air as I stared into the darkness.

Benedict snorted awake next to me, palm on my thigh. "Babe? What's wrong?"

My heart pounded as I stared into the dim surroundings. His bed. In his bedroom. In his apartment. Safe. My chest heaved and I fought to slow my breathing. It felt so real. I'd been paralyzed, lost in that dark water with not even a shred of hope to drag me to the surface.

"I dreamed I was — back there," I whispered, shivering.

"It's okay." His arm slid around my waist and dragged me down next to him so he could spoon me close. He kissed the back of my neck. "You're safe."

I almost didn't dare blink.

Benedict stroked from my waist and down my hip to my thigh, over and over, then his hand began to wander elsewhere. A delicious heat ignited in my stomach and drove away some of the fear and ice weighing me down. I rolled so I could face him and plant my lips on his.

He laughed, then kissed me back until I lay breathless half-under him. He traced shapes on my clavicle, nuzzling behind my ear. "I want to give you another shower. Make you smell like me even more."

I kissed his jaw and the corner of his mouth, my hands more bold on his sides. Not quite desperate but almost. I touched his stomach and let my palm slide down and down until I found his hard length standing between us.

Benedict sucked in a breath and caught my shoulders, holding me back for a moment. "Are you sure you're ready, Eloise? You just came back this morning and —"

"I'm still cold," I said. I stroked his velvety cock and pulled a groan from him as well. "I want to be warm everywhere, Benedict. Inside and out. Warm me up. Please."

He rumbled in his chest and grabbed my hips, kneading my butt until I arched my back and gripped his hair. His mouth left a searing trail to my breasts, drawing on my nipples until I cried out and tried to pull him closer, pushing my hips at him. I wanted him inside me, moving on top of me. Driving me towards that cliff of pleasure that would fix everything.

"Tell me what you want," Benedict said as he knelt over me, all dark and mysterious in the shadows of his bedroom. He gripped my thighs and his eyes devoured every inch of me until I flushed and squirmed under his survey.

"I want you to hold me," I said. I caught his face and dragged his lips to mine, then wrapped my legs around his hips. "Make me feel again."

The grumble turned into a purr. He lay on his side and drew my leg over his hip, murmuring, "Nice and easy, baby," as the blunt head of his cock slid against my channel.

I gasped again and held still as he pressed forward, the thick length parting me in an inevitable push. My head fell back on the pillow and stars sparked in my vision. Benedict's hand slid into my hair and drew my head to his shoulder, keeping me close, and he began to rock his hips to mine. I shivered and shook in his arms with the gentle thrusts, the crush of my breasts against his chest, the nipping at my shoulder.

Heat traveled from my core to every part of me, thawing the rest of the darkness that lurked inside me, and I held on to him desperately as I tried to move faster. But he kept up the gentle, steady rocking until I clawed at his back and my muscles clamped down on his invading cock. I moaned, pressing my face against his neck, and he grumbled in pleasure.

Sweat covered us both and made a slick friction where our bodies met. I sighed and tensed against him as he continued his slow torment, rocking into me as he teased my sides and kissed my throat and loved every inch of me. Everywhere he touched me, I burned with fierce desire. He ignited strength in me, until I felt powerful and invincible and protected. Loved.

I cried out as another wave of ecstasy rolled over me and Benedict groaned, his movements short and sharp and deep as he found his own pleasure. The hot rush of his climax filled me as well and I clung to him, hitching my leg higher on his hip as I tried to pull him deeper, keep his stomach pressed to mine.

Benedict sighed as he kissed a trail from my shoulder to my lips, stroking my hip in appreciation. "I love you, Eloise."

"I love you," I said to his throat, even as fatigue rolled over me and I wanted to sleep.

"Are you warm enough?"

It sounded like he was laughing at me, but I didn't care. I nodded and stretched. "Good job, Bennie."

"Don't ever call me Bennie," he murmured, kissing my forehead. He rolled to his back but took me with him, until I sprawled across his chest. The purr vibrated through me and I stretched. He traced the path of my backbone from my shoulders to my butt over and over, as if he petted me, and I settled more closely against his body.

Benedict pulled the sheets and comforter up over us but kept me cradled on his chest so he could wrap his arms around me. I set my teeth to his earlobe and said very quietly, "I'll call you whatever I want, Bennie."

His smile curved against my cheek and I smiled back. He patted my butt — not quite a spank, but a harbinger of good times to come. "For now, you naughty girl."

I dozed. The rhythm of his heart and the even rise and fall of his chest lulled me. But when I dreamed and thought I might be paralyzed, the sound of his heart drew me back to safety. To warmth. To love.

epilogue

A week later, I still didn't feel entirely myself. Periodically vertigo would wash over me and I would have to brace against something solid until the world stopped swirling and the feeling returned to my hands and feet. Luckily Benedict was always near, and solid and warm to lean into. He didn't endear himself by insisting I face the city prosecutor at the courthouse to deal with some of those pesky criminal charges I thought I'd outrun.

But I went, wearing business clothes that Natalia pronounced made me look "almost respectable." Benedict went with me, and Carter lumbered along with us as extra help in case I had an "episode" and needed to be hidden or rushed away. He also gave me encouraging smiles as I limped into the courthouse and Benedict whistled and swung his arms like he was playing hooky.

The prosecutor was an older woman with half-moon glasses on the end of her nose and an expansive coif of gray hair reminiscent of an earlier decade. But her steel gray eyes, the same shade as her hair, cut right through me. "You've been quite busy, Ms. Deacon. Imagine my surprise to hear Mr. Chase is representing you."

"Serendipity?" I said. The chairs in front of her desk were uncomfortable but I didn't dare move to ease the pain in my back; I got the feeling she might chastise me for fidgeting and I'd end up back in jail.

Her lips pursed. She directed an arch look at Benedict. "And you, Mr. Chase. I've never known you to do pro bono work."

"Serendipity," he said with a grin, as innocent and sunshiny as a boy scout.

The woman, Geralyn Mastriano, did not look charmed by handsome Benedict. Her fingers drummed on the surface of her battered desk, and I started to panic. She could throw me right back into jail for whatever she wanted, and even Benedict's perfect white teeth and fat wallet full of cash wouldn't get me out. Geralyn moved the glasses higher up on her nose and studied my file. "I heard you had some health problems recently, Ms. Deacon. I'm sorry to hear that. I also heard these health problems changed your world outlook and you're no longer going to be engaging in illegal pursuits. Is this true?"

"Yes ma'am," I said.

She made an unimpressed noise in her throat and watched me over the tops of her glasses. "If I agree to plea this down and give you community service, Ms. Deacon, where would you do that service?"

"A soup kitchen, ma'am." I winced and moved in the chair, hoping the pins and needles in my butt were due to the hard plastic and not getting re-paralyzed. "The same one I used to

Layla Nash

have to go to. I know what it's like to be there. I want to show them what it's like to get past it, to move forward. Move up."

I hadn't told Benedict that part; I didn't dare look at him directly, but in my peripheral vision, his expression softened. Looked like he wanted to hug me right there. The prosecutor did not look similarly impressed. She paged through the file. "And how do you propose to support yourself?"

"A receptionist at a gym. It's a new gym." I cleared my throat, hand flapping nervously in Benedict's general direction. "Some of Mr. Chase's friends are opening a gym and asked me to be the receptionist and do odd jobs around the place."

"I'm sure Mr. Chase's friends are doing all kinds of things these days."

Benedict put his hand over his heart. "Geralyn, you wound me. I'm just a good samaritan, trying to help a misguided little lamb find her way through a treacherous —"

"Mr. Chase," the prosecutor said, but her lips twitched in something like a smile. The first hint of any emotion other than irritation. "While I'm sure you're perfectly altruistic in your support for this young lady, the court does not have quite your enthusiasm for Ms. Deacon's potential. She's been a petty criminal for some time without any hint of remorse. So. Rather than expunge your record entirely, Ms. Deacon, you and I will make a deal. You will complete three hundred hours of community service. You will hold down a full time job. You will report in to your parole officer every week in person. At the end of three months, we will meet to evaluate your progress. If you're on the straight and narrow, I'll close out your case and you'll be free to continue your life as you please. So long as it's legal."

She fixed me with a hard look and jabbed her finger in my direction. "But if you violate any of these conditions, Ms. Deacon, I will come after you with everything I have, do you understand? I know you worked for Val Szdoka, and though she disappeared under questionable circumstances, I've no doubt there are many more skeletons in your closet than we see here," and she dropped the file on her desk. "And believe me, child, Benedict Chase doesn't make me even slightly nervous. You would need Jesus himself defending you to have a chance of remaining a free woman."

I blinked, leaning back in my chair without thinking. Holy shit on toast. That woman was terrifying. "Y-yes ma'am. I don't think I can afford Jesus's retainer."

"You can't afford Benedict Chase's, either," she said under her breath. Geralyn scowled at Benedict, who grinned glee-fully next to me, not at all perturbed by her speech. "And you, young man. Do not cross me. I will absolutely call your brother if I see you shirking or leading Ms. Deacon astray."

"Geralyn," he said, holding his hands up. "I promise, Logan is also —"

"I will call your mother if I have to," she said, glasses once more on the end of her nose as she frowned at him. Benedict went still next to me, the color draining from his face as she went on, each word slow and deliberate and meant to terrify. "I've no doubt she would have a strong opinion on this matter."

"Yes ma'am," he said.

I stared at him, mouth gaping. Benedict Chase, huge shifter lion and powerhouse corporate lawyer, lost his devil-may-care attitude the moment she brought up his mother? And how the hell did the prosecutor know his mother?

"Very well." Geralyn stacked the papers on her desk and directed her attention to me. "Do we have a deal, Ms. Deacon?"

"Yes ma'am." I nodded, half a second away from curtseying or rolling over to show her my belly.

"Good. I will see you in three months." She rose from behind her desk and I scrambled to my feet. Geralyn briefly shook my hand, then gave me a final stern look over her glasses. "You'd better be on your best behavior, young lady, or I will hear about it and you will *both* answer to me."

She frowned at Benedict as she shook his hand, then added, "Give my best to Esther."

"Yes ma'am," he said.

I waited until we were in the hallway to smack his arm. "She knows your *mother*?"

"Hush," he said, putting his arm around my waist to guide me out of the building. "You'll ruin my reputation around here. I can't let anyone know my mother is the most terrifying person on the planet."

Carter grinned as he fell in behind us, hands shoved in his pockets. I glanced at him and he shook his head. "She's a lovely woman. Just doesn't like practical jokes," and Carter sent a significant look at his brother.

I laughed, delighted, and almost tripped in my glee as Benedict opened a door and we were outside in the chilly air. He held me close to his side and bent to kiss the top of my head. "I don't know what he's talking about, I was an absolute angel as a boy."

And I'd believe that right after I met the tooth fairy. By Carter's snort, doubt was the correct response. I leaned into him as we walked slowly away from the courthouse, down an almost-familiar street. "How does she know your mother?"

Benedict dropped his wounded expression. "Geralyn is a badger."

"A what?" I stopped in my tracks and looked back at the courthouse.

"A werebadger," Benedict said. He smiled, and held my face in his hands as he pressed his lips to mine. "She's tenacious as fuck, too. No one crosses Geralyn. Even the loan sharks won't dare pop up on her radar."

"A badger," I said under my breath, and shook my head. So I would definitely have to be on my best behavior. She meant every word of her threat.

"Yep." Benedict kissed me again, slower, and as I melted against him, humming with pleasure as he kindled heat all the way through me, Carter cleared his throat. Benedict glanced at his brother, still kissing me, and managed to say with half his mouth, "Give me a break, dude."

Carter rolled his eyes and pulled out his phone. "I'll call Edgar for a ride. Congratulations, Eloise," and he walked away with a long-suffering sigh.

Benedict nibbled on my lips as his hand pressed to the small of my back and drew me close. My knees weakened and I linked my arms around him. He chuckled. "I like you in those fancy clothes, looking all prim and proper. I want to take them all off you, of course."

"Maybe you should," I murmured, and played with his tie.

"I promised to buy you lunch." Benedict canted his head at the restaurant right next to him, Bistro Nord, where we'd eaten together that first day. "And this time I want to make it all the way to dessert."

I bit my lower lip as I looked up at him and nestled my hips to his. I pushed my hair back and went up on my toes to whisper in his ear. "Are you sure?"

"Maybe we'll get dessert to go. They'll box it up for us." He groaned as I kissed his jaw, and he squeezed my butt to draw me closer. "We can skip the salad. It's terrible. Vegetables are rubbish."

I laughed and drew away, tugging on his hand to guide him toward the restaurant. "Well, if we have the salad, we might need to take a break in the middle. I certainly might need to excuse myself." As he pulled me back suddenly and crushed me to his chest, I added, "And if you meet me in the bathroom, we can have dessert early."

The purr rumble started in his chest and he kissed me, hard. I closed my eyes and relaxed against him. I finally felt warm all the way through. Every time he touched me, I felt alive. Benedict drew back but kept me close as he headed to the restaurant and the polite doorman with averted eyes. My lion leaned to murmur in my ear, "Maybe we have dessert before the soup, and then after the salad, and then we take the chocolate mousse to go so we can have dessert at home. Twice."

I laughed, cheeks on fire, and headed straight for the bathroom as Benedict chatted with the maître d'. If we locked the door, he could hold me up against the wall and we'd have plenty of time and room in the super fancy bathroom. I shivered in ecstasy, ready for him as I heard the heavy tread of his steps approaching. I unbuttoned my skirt.

Maybe not entirely on my best behavior.

Chasing Trouble

a sneak peak:

storm chaser

Atticus wiped blood off his face and threw the towel aside. He paced the confines of the small prep room reserved for fighters. Two fights down and he needed a third to make sure the lion remained calm and quiet the next few days. The constant struggle for control wore him down; fighting was the only thing that helped. And lately Edgar watched him with a hint of suspicion, as if he knew that Atticus struggled.

Atticus glanced up as one of the organizers, a skinny dude from the coyote pack, slid past the door and eyed him up and down. "You looking for another?"

"Yeah." Atticus poked at his nose, hoping it set correctly as the shifter healing kicked in.

"I've got a good one." The coyote grinned and slapped him on the back. "Easy one for you, mate. A girl."

"Not a chance." He shook his head and started packing his bag. "No way in hell. I don't hit girls."

"It pays. Five grand to go one round. Take a couple of swings."

"No." A growl boiled up in his chest and Atticus loomed over the much smaller, much skinnier coyote.

The other man backed up, hands raised. "Okay, okay. That's it for tonight, though. The kid's a champion. She could probably kick your ass anyway."

Atticus just shook his head and picked up the bag. "Like I said. No fucking way."

"Is this him?" a cheerful voice piped up from the door, and a woman poked her head in to eye Atticus.

She might as well have punched him in the chest. Atticus could only stare at her. Tall and athletic but with inviting curves hidden by sweaty workout gear, the girl eyed him like a mountain to climb. The coyote, John, shrugged. "Sorry, Soph. He won't go for it."

"Come on." She eased into the room and leaned back against the door, her full lips curving into an encouraging smile. "Five grand for each of us for a couple of minutes? Come on, big guy. You can take a swing at me for that, right?"

"I don't hit women." Atticus took a deep breath and her scent coiled around his brain — more so because she'd had at least one fight earlier and smelled of perspiration and a little bit of violence. His lion grumbled and strained against his control, wanting to get much, much closer to the woman. "I don't even pretend to hit women. Or play like I hit women. Sorry."

"John, can you give us a minute?" She didn't take her eyes off Atticus, though, and he unconsciously flexed until his shoulders grew. The coyote left, still hopeful, and Atticus braced himself for some kind of proposition. Instead, she held out a hand expertly wrapped for boxing. "I'm Sophia, by the way."

"Atticus." He barely pressed her fingers in his, not wanting to leave a trace of himself on her. At least until he could rub his face in her hair.

"Atticus?" She smiled as she repeated his name, and he braced himself for the teasing. Instead, she bit her lower lip prettily. "Look, Atticus. I need the money. It's one round and it pays more than everything else I've earned tonight. Please? We get paid regardless of who wins."

He still shook his head. His stomach turned over at the thought of facing her in the makeshift ring, the crowd jeering and calling for blood. She might get hurt. He was a big clumsy dude normally, and if he slipped, if he accidentally made contact... Jesus. He could knock her skull in and kill her.

Her red hair, captured tightly in some intricate braid thing, shone as she leaned closer and into the light from a single bare bulb. "Come on. I'll let you win."

His mouth twitched. He sighed, scrubbing his hands over his face. "One round. But I'm not going to hit you."

Sophia turned on her heel and bounced toward the door. "Sure you won't."

He followed, still shaking his head. This was a bad idea. He just knew it. But her ass was a pleasant distraction as she led the way. The lion breathed *Want her* in his mind and Atticus had to look away before the rest of his control fled with his good sense.

The crowd seethed around the plywood borders of the ring, but they made way as John and then Sophia headed for the bare ground. Atticus shuffled after them, looking around the abandoned warehouse, and rubbed his jaw. She smelled good, and not just because she was hot and sweaty and amped up on adrenaline. She wasn't human. Probably feline, but not a lion. The tumult of the crowd increased as he stepped past the plywood gate and one of the bouncers slapped his shoulder. "Go get her. Put her in her place, Atticus."

He bared his teeth at the shithead. Like Atticus would beat her down just because someone convinced her to get in the ring with a man. Women were to be protected, sheltered, cared for and loved. Not hurt. Not mocked. A snarl built in his chest and he had to take a moment to compose himself lest the lion decide to attack the heckler. He cracked his knuckles and paced around the perimeter of the ring. She stood in the center, watching him, as John announced the fight and a flurry of bets changed hands. When his bookie gestured for Atticus to place a wager, Atticus waved him off.

John scrambled out of the ring and Sophia held her fists up to guard her face as the bell rang. Any hint of a cheerful girl dropped from her expression and a predator faced him. Atticus's eyebrows rose, and he put his guard up as well as she flew at him. She landed a flurry of blows against his kidneys, then kicked out his knee to try to get him on the ground. Atticus blocked and dodged, distracted and mesmerized by the beauty and simplicity of her fighting technique. She was efficient and capable, faster than he'd thought. No wonder she was a champion.

The crowd roared, screaming for blood, and Atticus took a gentle swing at her. She dodged and landed a right hook to his chin that knocked him back a couple steps. She winked at him.

The lion loved her. The lion wanted her, roared and pushed to take control so they could finish the fight and take her home

Chasing Trouble

and protect her, somewhere the bloodthirsty assholes watching the fight would never find her. Tackle her and cover her with his scent. He dipped to avoid another vicious hook and she snapped a jab right through his guard. A flurry of kicks followed and he staggered, the crowd blurry.

She was amazing. His heart pounded and it had nothing to do with the exertion of fighting.

Her guard dropped for a split second and his instincts took over. He eased a hook toward her with his left, pulling it until only a fraction of his strength connected with her jaw, and she grunted, an *Oof* escaping that damn near broke his heart. He straightened from his fighting stance and lurched forward to check if she was okay.

A roar cut through the pheromone fog in his brain and Atticus's stomach dropped. Logan. The distraction had him looking up, and then back at Sophia — well, at her fist. He didn't register what came first: the sidekick to his gut or the roundhouse to his head.

He was still staring at her in befuddled amazement as he hit the floor.

About the Author

Thank you for reading! I hope you enjoyed the City Shifters books. If you'd like to be notified of new releases, please join my mailing list by going to EEPURL.COM/BWQz3X

Please feel free to email me directly at
LAYLARNASH@YAHOO.COM

or check out my website at
LAYLANASH.COM.

If you enjoyed the book, please take a moment to leave a review. I'd love to hear from you!

Thanks!
Layla

Also by Layla Nash

Printed in Great Britain
by Amazon